IN DIAMOND SQUARE

Mercè Rodoreda

Translated from Catalan
by Peter Bush

virago

VIRAGO

First published in Catalan with the title *La plaça del Diamant* in 1962
This edition first published in hardback in Great Britain in 2013 by Virago Press
This paperback edition published in 2014 by Virago Press

3 5 7 9 10 8 6 4 2

The translation of this work was supported by a grant from the Institut Ramon Llull.

 **institut
ramon llull**
Catalan Language and Culture

A CIP catalogue record for this book
is available from the British Library.

ISBN 978-1-84408-737-2

Typeset in Goudy by M Rules
Printed and bound in Great Britain by
Clays Ltd, St Ives plc

Papers used by Virago are from well-managed forests
and other responsible sources.

MIX
Paper from
responsible sources
FSC
www.fsc.org   FSC® C104740

Virago Press
An imprint of
Little, Brown Book Group
Carmelite House
50 Victoria Embankment
London EC4Y 0DZ

An Hachette UK Company
www.hachette.co.uk

www.virago.co.uk

VIRAGO MODERN CLASSICS

572

Mercè Rodoreda

Mercè Rodoreda i Gurguí (1908–83) was born and raised in Barcelona. In 1928 she married and in 1929 her only son, Jordi, was born. She began writing fiction and published her prize-winning first novel, *Aloma*, in the 1930s. At the outbreak of the Spanish Civil War in July 1936 Rodoreda was working for the Generalitat de Catalunya, the region's autonomous government, and when the Generalitat was suppressed by General Franco she sought exile in France and later Switzerland, where she remained until the 1970s. In 1957, she broke her silence with the prize-winning short story collection *Vint-i-dos contes*, and in 1962 published *In Diamond Square* (*La plaça del Diamant*). It became the most highly acclaimed Catalan novel of modern times and has been translated into more than twenty languages. Her books also include *El carrer de les Camèlies* (1966), *Jardí vora el mar* (1967), *Mirall trencat* (1974), *Viatges i flors*, *Quanta, quanta guerra* (1980) and *La mort i la primavera*. In 1980 she was awarded Catalunya's highest literary honour, the Premi d'honor de les Lletres Catalanes, and in 1998 the Mercè Rodoreda literary prize for short stories and narratives was established in her honour. She died in Girona, Catalunya.

For J.P.

My dear, these things are life.
Meredith

PROLOGUE

In Diamond Square begins: 'Julie came to the cake-shop just to tell me they would be raffling coffeepots before they got to the lucky posy; she'd seen them and they were lovely, an orange split in two, showing its pips, painted on a white background.' When I was writing this opening sentence I hadn't the slightest idea that so many editions in Catalan and so many translations of my novel would be published.

When writing the novel I could hardly remember what the real Diamond Square was like. I could only recall how at the age of thirteen or fourteen I once wandered the streets of Gràcia with my father during the annual fiestas. They had erected a marquee in Diamond Square. In other squares as well, but that is the one I always remembered most. When I walked past that musical box, I was desperate to join the dance, but my parents had forbidden me to dance, and I walked those festive streets like a soul in purgatory. Perhaps that frustration was to blame for the fact I started the novel with that marquee years later in Geneva.

I am a child of Sant Gervasi de Cassoles, a short, narrow street that at the time ran from Pàdua to the gully in Sant Gervasi that was then called Sant Anton, later París and even later Manuel Angelón, which is still its name today. Sant Gervasi isn't far from Gràcia. I knew the area because I went to matinées at the Trilla, Smart and Mundial cinemas with my grandfather. I knew the Santa Isabel market because at the age of four or five I went there with a neighbour on summer afternoons to buy fish, after we had crossed the stream called the Olla. Between the ages of fifteen and seventeen, and for a long time after, I would often stroll down the High Street in Gràcia with my mother. We would reach it from the Rambla del Prat, walk down as far as the gardens and walk back up the pavement on the other side. We were window-shopping.

I only have warm memories of Gràcia. That is all very distant now, but I think of them, on a wave of nostalgia, and feel good; I have found great consolation in these memories on many occasions and in very different circumstances.

I would like all those who read my novel to share those feelings of mine. I am very pleased that among the thousands of readers there are many who have never read anything in Catalan and that by reading it they have discovered ours is a civilised, cultured and important language. I am very pleased that this simple, human novel has taken the name of Diamond Square in the district of Gràcia and with it the name of Catalonia to so many distant countries.

I have never been very enthusiastic about writing prologues, or speaking about myself (or my work, which amounts to the same thing).

It might perhaps be interesting to explain the genesis of *In Diamond Square*, but can you in fact explain how a novel is shaped, what impulses spark it off, what strength of will enables it to be sustained, the struggle to finish what is so easily begun? Would it be enough to say the idea came to me in Geneva when I was gazing at the mountain of Salève or walking around Perle-du-Lac park? I can say, and it is partly true, that *In Diamond Square* was prompted by a disappointment.

I had submitted *Garden by the Sea* for the Joanot Martorell Prize (the last time it was awarded) and the jury didn't like it. This upset provoked an unnatural reaction in me; I have always been stimulated by obstacles. I started another novel, driven by a surge of pride.

Quite absurdly, I wanted it to be Kafkaesque, very Kafka-esque – with lots of pigeons. I wanted the pigeons to overwhelm the protagonist from start to finish. So I conceived what eventually became *In Diamond Square*, before I ever sat down behind a typewriter next to a pile of paper and wrote feverishly, as if each day I worked on the novel were the last of my life.

I worked as if in a trance. Every afternoon I corrected what I had written in the morning, trying to ensure that, despite the speed at which I was writing, my horse didn't get out of control, and I kept a firm grip on the reins so it didn't lose its way. Some people speak of narrative explosions. I cannot think what that means. To write a novel, which is a work requiring concentration, one has to be calm and very self-possessed.

And the novel that started out as a nightmare about pigeons changed into *In Diamond Square*, still with pigeons, but in a very different sense. It was a time of great nervous tension and left me quite sick. In due course, *In Diamond Square* was entered for the first Sant Jordi Prize for literature and received the same treatment as *Garden by the Sea* in the final Joanot Martorell.

*

When the novel was published, my friend Baltasar Porcel was full of praise but he said that the main character, Pidgey, was a simple soul. I think this rather light-hearted affirmation is entirely mistaken. To see the world through the eyes of a child, in a constant state of wonder, is not tantamount to being a simple soul, quite the contrary. Moreover, Pidgey does what she must do within the situation she finds herself in, and to do what must be done and no more reveals a natural talent that deserves the greatest respect. I believe that Pidgey is more intelligent than Madame Bovary or Anna Karenina, and nobody has ever dreamed of calling them simple souls. Perhaps that is because they were rich, wore silk and had servants. And although, when I was young, I dreamed of being Madame Bovary or Anna Karenina – the latter rather than the former – when I needed a central character for my novel I chose Pidgey, who has only one thing in common with me, namely the fact that she feels at a loss in the midst of the world.

Writers have always spoken about things in novels (about furniture, the hands and pendulums of clocks, paintings, the shape and colour of armchairs and settees, of oil-lamps and standard lamps, of royal carpets and canopies). From Balzac to Proust via Tolstoi, to mention the ones who have made the most impact. Things are very important in narrative and always have been. Long before Robbe-Grillet ever wrote *Le voyeur*. Things abound in *In Diamond Square*: the funnel, the conch-shell, the dolls in the emporium ... there is much detail about the furniture, doorbells and doors of the house where Pidgey goes to work. There are the gold coins Father John gives Joe in case they are hard up. There are the scales etched on the staircase wall. And a sexual symbol, the knife, with which, at the end of the novel, Pidgey inscribes her name on the door of the house where she once lived.

However, there are not merely objects in the novel, there is above all the character of Pidgey. She was suggested to me by a protagonist of a short story I wrote some time before, *Afternoon at the Movies*, which is in the collection *Twenty-two Stories* and was inspired by Voltaire's *Candide*. If Voltaire hadn't written *Candide* it is quite possible *In Diamond Square* might never have seen the light of day. And what about the influence of James Joyce? Perhaps the conclusion to my novel comes from the famous monologue in *Ulysses*. But I think it would be more accurate to look for the source of chapter XXIII of *In Diamond Square*, the one about the death of Joe's mother, in some of the stories in *The Dubliners*.

If I hadn't read Bernat Metge, I would never have decided to have Pidgey give that physical description of her brand-new husband.* Bernat Metge has Ovid describe the delights of his beloved; this chapter, perfect in its style and language, is called 'Description of the lass'. A few pages that are among the best in world literature. The 'Description of the lass' by Bernat Metge gave me the idea of the 'description of the lad', in other words of Joe, that the reader will find in chapter VIII of my novel. I thank Bernat Metge for giving me more than I deserve. And I offer him my humblest apologies for the liberty I have taken.

I would have to admit to many other influences; everything I have read, with the Bible in pride of place. I want to state that *In Diamond Square* is a novel about love, as someone has said that it isn't. Many novels have been written about love. From the most spiritual and chivalresque to the most carnal love, the

---

* Translator's note: Bernat Metge, *Lo somni* (1399): in this humanistic dialogue, Metge writes about the vices and virtues of women and pens a detailed, sensually physical description of a beautiful maiden.

latter being represented by one of the most trite novels possible, over which so much ink has been spilt, by a great writer, D. H. Lawrence. I am referring to *Lady Chatterley's Lover*. But the tenderest, most delicate love story is that of Francesca da Rimini in Canto V of *Hell*, in the *Divine Comedy*.* A story that begins with these wonderful lines:

> The town sits where I was born
> on the coast, where Po runs down
> with his streams to final peace.

And Ulysses' love, not for Penelope, not for charming Nausicaa, but his passionate love of adventure. In Canto XXVI of *Hell*, Dante sends him with four old and rickety friends, in a leaky boat, on the final adventure: the adventure of death.

> Neither joy in a son, nor my duty
> to an aged father, nor the love
> I owed to Penelope's happiness,
> none could beat the thirst in me
> to be wise in the ways of men,
> to know their strengths and sins . . .

Apart from Dante and the Bible, among the books that have most marked me and that I want to mention here, I should name Homer.

*

* Translator's note: English translation by Steve Ellis, *Dante Hell* (Chatto & Windus, 1994).

I now want to repeat, because it pains me that someone should deny it: I want to affirm vehemently that *In Diamond Square* is above all a novel of love, though it contains not à scrap of sentimentality. The moment when Pidgey returns from the death of her past, walks into her house at dawn and embraces her second husband, the man who had saved her from all the miseries of life, is a scene of profound love. 'I thought how I didn't want him to die on me ...' Then she puts her finger in his belly button so 'no witch could suck him dry through his belly button and take my Anthony away from me ... ' And it isn't by chance that the last word in the novel is 'Happy'. I didn't use it on a whim. It suggests that, although so much sadness exists in life, a little cheerfulness can be life-saving. A few birds, for example, 'and inside each puddle, however small, there would be a sky ... the sky a bird sometimes disturbed ... a thirsty bird disturbing the sky unawares with water from its beak ... or shrieking out of the foliage like flashes of lightning, several birds would swoop down for a quick bath in the puddle, ruffling their feathers and then wiping the mud, their beaks and their wings all over the sky. Happy ... '

In Diamond Square is far from me now. As if I never wrote it. Very far. Now, when I am about to finish this prologue, I am concerned with my garden. My pale pink Prunus and my small coral-pink Jupiter tree are flowering. The north wind is rising and will batter them. I must go and see what the wind and the flowers are doing.

Mercè Rodoreda
Romanyà de la Selva, 1982

I

Julie came to the cake-shop just to tell me they would be raffling coffeepots before they got to the lucky posy; she'd seen them and they were lovely, an orange split in two, showing its pips, painted on a white background. I didn't feel like going to the dance or even going out, after I'd spent the whole day selling cakes and my fingertips ached from tying all those gilded raffia knots and handles. And because I knew Julie could manage on as little as three hours' sleep and didn't mind whether she slept or not. But she insisted I went all the same, and that was me all over, it upset me when I was asked to do something and had to say no. I went in white from head to toe: starched dress and petticoat, shoes like splashes of milk, white paste earrings, three matching bangles and a white handbag Julie said was oilskin, with a clasp like a golden seashell.

The musicians had started playing by the time we reached the square. The roof was decorated with flowers and brightly coloured streamers made from paper and flowers. Some of the flowers were wrapped round light bulbs and the whole roof was like an inside out umbrella, with the streamers attached right at the top, not halfway down. The elastic holding my petticoat up felt too tight. I'd struggled to thread it through with a crochet hook that kept snagging, and now a little button and loop of cotton were holding it in place. I pictured the red weal round my waist, but the moment I started rushing and getting out of breath, the elastic sliced into me again. The platform where the musicians had struck up was surrounded by banks of asparagus fern that, bedecked with artificial flowers, served as a barrier. The musicians, in their shirtsleeves, were sweating. My mother died years ago and wasn't there to give me advice, and my father had remarried. He found a second wife and I'd lost a mother who only lived to look after me. My father remarried and here I was, a young girl, alone in Diamond Square, waiting for them to start raffling coffeepots, with Julie shouting trying to make herself heard above the music, stop or you'll get in a right state! and me gawping at the flower-bedecked light bulbs, the streamers glued down with water and flour and everybody enjoying themselves, and me all eyes, when a voice in my ear whispered, want to dance?

And not really thinking I replied I didn't know how and turned round to take a look. I found a face so close to mine I couldn't really see what it was like, that it was a young man's. Don't worry, he said, I do and I'll soon teach you. I thought of poor Pete in his white apron shut up in the basement cooking at the Columbus Hotel, and blurted out: 'And what if my fiancé finds out?'

The young man moved even closer and laughed, 'Aren't you too young to have a fiancé?' And when he laughed, his lips parted and I could see all his teeth. He had little monkey eyes and wore a blue-striped white shirt, open at the collar, and his armpits were soaked with sweat. And he suddenly turned his back on me, stood on tiptoe, swung round again, swayed this way and that, and said, sorry, and shouted: 'Hey? Anyone seen my jacket? It was on a chair next to the musicians! Hey!' And he said someone had stolen his jacket and he'd be back straight away and he hoped I'd wait. He started shouting: 'Ernie! Ernie!'

All green-embroidered canary yellow, Julie appeared from nowhere and said, hide me, I've just got to take these shoes off . . . I can't dance another step . . . I told her I couldn't budge because a young man who was looking for his jacket wanted to dance with me and had begged me to wait. And Julie said, you dance, you dance . . . And it was so hot. Kids were letting off rockets and bangers on street corners. The ground was strewn with watermelon seeds, and peel and empty beer bottles were stacked in the corners of the square and they were letting off rockets from roof terraces and balconies. I could see sweaty faces and the boys wiping their faces with their handkerchiefs. The musicians were swinging gleefully. All like a stage set. And then the *paso doble*. I danced up and down and he seemed a long way away, even though he was really very close, whispering, look how well she dances! And a strong whiff of sweat and stale eau de cologne hit me and I was eyeball to eyeball with his sparkling monkey eyes and little medal-like ears. And that elastic cutting into my waist and my mother dead and gone and not around to give me advice, because I told him my boyfriend was a cook at the Columbus and he laughed and said he was very sorry for his sake because I'd be his wife and darling within a year. And we'd dance the lucky posy dance in Diamond Square.

He said, my darling.

And said I'd be his wife within a year and I'd not even taken a good look at him, and now I did and he said, don't stare at me like that, or they'll have to pick me up off the floor, and that was when I told him he'd got monkey eyes and he laughed till he cried. The elastic round my waist cut into me like a knife and the musicians, tra-la-la, tra-lee-lee. And Julie was nowhere to be seen. She'd vanished. And his eyes looked deep into mine as if the whole world was in them and there was no escape. And the night sped on under the Great Bear in the sky, and the party sped on and the girl in blue with the posy whirled round and round ... My mother six feet under in Sant Gervasi and me here in Diamond Square ... Are they selling anything sweet? Honey and glazed fruit? And the exhausted musicians putting their things away in their cases, then taking them out again because a neighbour had just paid for one more waltz and everybody spinning like tops. When the waltz ended people began to leave. I said I'd lost Julie and he said he'd lost Ernie and, when we were all alone, and everyone was in bed and the streets empty, he said, you and I will dance a dawn waltz in Diamond Square ... round and round ... Pidgey. I looked at him taken aback and told him my name was Natalia and when I said my name was Natalia he laughed again and said there could be only one name for me: Pidgey. That was when I broke into a run and he chased me, don't be scared ... don't you see you can't walk down these streets by yourself, somebody will steal you from me? And he grabbed my arm and stopped me in my tracks, don't you see somebody will steal you away, Pidgey? And my mother dead and me stuck there with the elastic cutting deep into my waist like a piece of wire tying me to a frond of asparagus fern.

And I started running again. With him in hot pursuit. The

shops had pulled their shutters down over windows full of things that stood stock-still, inkpots, blotting paper and postcards and displays of dolls and clothes, aluminium pans and knitted goods . . . And we came out on to the High Street, me in front, him chasing, and both running at top speed, and, years later, Pidgey, he'd still tell the story, the day I met her in Diamond Square, she ran away at full tilt and right by the tram stop, her petticoat dropped to the ground!

The cotton broke and my petticoat dropped. I jumped over it, almost tripped and ran as if all the devils in hell were at my heels. I got home and threw myself on my bed in the dark, on my little girl's brass bed, as if I was hurling a stone at it. I was so ashamed. When I got over my shame, I kicked my shoes off and let my hair down. And, years later, Joe still told the story as if it had happened yesterday, her elastic snapped and she ran like the wind . . .

II

It was all very mysterious. I was wearing my dress the colour of rosewood which was on the skimpy side for the weather and getting goose pimples waiting for Joe on the street corner. After I'd been loafing around for a bit, I felt somebody was staring at me from behind a trellis shutter because I saw it move on one side. Joe and I had agreed to meet by Parc Güell. A small kid came out of one entrance, a revolver tucked in his belt, firing his rifle, and he brushed past my skirt shouting, bang . . . bang.

The trellis parted, the shutter opened wide and a young man in pyjamas went psst . . . psst with his lips and beckoned to me to come over, hooking a finger at me. Just to be sure I pointed my finger at my chest, looked at him and whispered, me? He couldn't hear but he understood and nodded, and his face was so handsome, and I crossed to his side of the road. As soon as I was under his balcony the young man said, come in, we can have a little snooze together.

I flushed a thousand shades of red and moved away in a temper, especially at myself, and upset because I could feel that young man staring at my back and through my clothes at my skin. I stood so the young fellow couldn't see me, but I was afraid if I stayed half hidden like that, Joe wouldn't see me either. I was wondering what was in store, because it was the first time we'd met by a park and I'd done all sorts of silly things in the morning thinking about the afternoon because I was worried stiff. Joe'd said we should meet at half past three and didn't come until half past four, but I didn't say anything because I thought that maybe I'd misheard him and I was the one who'd got it wrong, and as he didn't offer a single word of apology ... I didn't dare tell him my feet were killing me because I'd been standing up so long in those leather shoes that got so hot, or that a young man had taken liberties with me. We started to walk up the hill, didn't exchange one miserable word and when we were right at the top I didn't feel cold any more and my skin was as smooth as ever. I wanted to tell him I'd split up with Pete, so we were all set. We sat on a stone bench in a far corner, between two leafy, spindly trees, and a blackbird kept flying low, from one tree to another, cheep-cheeping softly, rather hoarsely, and then we lost sight of it for a few minutes until it flew back out from under a tree, but we had our minds on other things while it kept dipping like that. I looked at Joe out of the corner of my eye and he was staring at the small houses in the distance. In the end, he asked, don't you find that bird a bit scary?

I said I really liked it and he said his mother had always told him birds that were black, even if they were blackbirds, brought bad luck. Whenever we met, after that first day in Diamond Square, Joe always pressed close to me and asked if I'd split up with Pete. And now he didn't and I couldn't think how to begin to tell him I'd told Pete it was all over between us. And it made me miserable when I did, because Pete acted like a lit match that had been snuffed out. And when I thought how I'd broken with Pete, I felt sad and it made me think I'd done something wrong. You know, I'd always acted naturally, and when I remembered the look on Pete's face, I felt wretched as if a little door from a nest of scorpions had opened and released the beasts into my previous peace of mind, and they were cavorting in my misery, stinging painfully, and the sting was spreading through my veins and turning my blood black. Because Pete's voice choked, his eyes glazed over and flickered, and he said I'd ruined his life. I'd turned him into a piece of dirt. And when Joe stared at the blackbird, he began to talk about Mr Gaudí, whom his father had met the day he was knocked over by a tram, and how his father was one of the people who'd taken him to hospital, poor old Mr Gaudí, such a nice man, and he'd died so horribly ... And nothing in the world could beat the Parc Güell and the Sagrada Familia and the wavy balconies of the Pedrera. I said they were very nice but far too many waves and sharp spikes as far I was concerned. He tapped my knee with the side of his hand and he hit me so sharply my leg shot into the air and he said if I wanted to be his wife I'd have to start liking every single thing he liked. He gave me a long sermon about men and women and their respective rights and when I managed to get a word in I asked, 'And what if I don't like something one *little* bit?'

'You've just got to, you don't have a clue.'

And again, sermon: a very long one. He talked about all kinds of people in his family: his parents, an uncle who owned a small chapel and a prayer stool, his grandparents and the mothers of Ferdinand and Isabel, the Catholic King and Queen who, according to him, were the ones who'd put us on the right road.

And then, although I didn't get him at first, because he kept mixing it up with everything else he was saying, he said, poor Mary … And he mentioned the mothers of Ferdinand and Isabel yet again and that perhaps we could get married soon because two friends of his were looking for a place for us. And he'd make furniture for me that would blow me sideways as soon as I saw it because it wasn't for nothing he was a carpenter like St Joseph and I was like the Mother of God.

And he said all this very cheerfully and I was still wondering what he'd meant when he'd said, poor Mary … and I was fading as quickly as the light of day and the blackbird kept dipping low from under one tree to the next and out again as if lots of blackbirds were busy flying around.

'I'll make a wardrobe that will do for both of us, from bottlewood, with a side for you and a side for me. And when I've furnished the flat, I'll make a cot for the baby.'

He told me he couldn't make his mind up about children. He liked to flit from one thing to another. The sun was setting and the shadows became blue and mysterious without the sun. And Joe talked about wood, about this wood and that, and what you could do with jacaranda, mahogany, oak, holm-oak … Right then, I've just remembered and will always remember, he kissed me, and the moment he kissed me I saw Our Lord hovering over his house, deep inside a billowing cloud, swathed in a mandarin orange fabric that had faded down one side, and Our Lord opened wide his arms, which were very long, grabbed the edges of the cloud and shut himself inside as if he was shutting himself inside a wardrobe.

'We shouldn't have come today.'

And he ran one kiss into another and the whole sky misted over. I could see the big cloud drifting away and other smaller clouds appeared and started to chase that billowing cloud, and Joe tasted of milky coffee. And he shouted, they're locking the park!

'How do you know?'

'Didn't you hear the whistle?'

We got up, the blackbird took fright and flew off, the breeze blew my skirt up ... and we walked down one path after another. A girl sitting on a tile-covered bench was picking her nose and wiping a finger over an eight-pronged star on the back of the seat. I told Joe her dress was the same colour as mine. He didn't reply. When we were out in the street I told him, look, people are still going in ... and he said don't worry, they'll soon get them out. We walked down nearby streets and just when I was about to tell him, you know, Pete and I have split up, he stopped suddenly, stood in front of me, grabbed my arms and looked at me as if I'd done something wicked, poor Mary ...

I almost said don't worry, tell me what's wrong with Mary ... But I didn't dare. He let go of my arms, walked downhill by my side, until we reached the crossroads of Diagonal and the Passeig de Gràcia. We started walking round another block, and my feet couldn't stagger another step. When we'd been walking for half an hour, he stopped, grabbed me by the arms again, under a street lamp, and when I thought he was going to say poor Mary again, and I was holding my breath in anticipation, he growled: 'If we hadn't walked down so quickly, from up the top there, with the blackbird and all that, who knows what might have happened! But don't you worry, one day I'll catch you and you won't know what's hit you!'

We went round the houses until eight o'clock, not saying a word, as if we'd been born dumb. When I was by myself, I looked up at the pitch-black sky. And you know ... it was all very mysterious ...

III

There he was on the corner of the street, what a surprise, on a day when I wasn't expecting him.

'I want you to stop working for that pastry-cook! I've heard all about how he chases after his shop girls.'

I started shaking and told him to stop shouting, that I couldn't leave my job just like that, so rudely, without a decent excuse, that the poor fellow never had an ill word to say about me, that I liked selling cakes and if he forced me give it up, what would I do ... He said that one dark, wintry afternoon, he'd come to see me at work. And he said that, when I was helping a customer to choose a box of chocolates from the right-hand window, the pastry-cook's eyes had trailed not after me, but after my behind. I told him not to be silly and that we might as well forget it if he couldn't trust me.

'I do trust you, but I don't want that pastry-cook having a good time at your expense.'

'You're mad,' I told him, 'he only ever thinks about his business! Get it?'

I was so angry my cheeks flushed a bright red. He grabbed me by the throat and shook my head. I told him to clear off and, if he didn't, I'd go to the police. We didn't see one another for three weeks and just when I was beginning to regret telling Pete it was all over between us, because at the end of the day Pete was a good lad who'd never been nasty to me, and was only a good worker who was crazy about his job, Joe turned up, cool as a cucumber, and the first thing he said, stuffing his hands into his pockets, was, poor Mary, sent packing because of you . . .

We went along Prat to the High Street. He stopped by the entrance to a grocery store that was full of sacks, put his hand in a sack of birdseed and said, what lovely seed . . . and we walked off again. He was holding some seed in his hand and when I wasn't looking he put it down the back of my blouse. He stopped me in front of a window full of clothes, see them? when we're married, I'll buy you some of those aprons and I said they looked straight out of the workhouse and he said they were what his mother used to wear and I said I couldn't care less, I wasn't going to wear them because they looked as shabby as you could get.

He said he'd introduce me to his mother, that he'd already told her about me and that his mother wanted to see for herself the girl her son had chosen. We went on a Sunday. She lived by herself. Joe lived in a lodging-house so as not to give her work and he said that made them more friends because they didn't get on at all well together. And his mother lived in a small house on the street with the flats for journalists and you could see the sea from her balcony and the mist that sometimes covered it. She was a very particular lady, proud of her elaborate permanent waves. Her house was full of ribbons and bows. Joe had told me all about them. There was a bow over the Holy Christ above her bed-head. It was a black mahogany bed with two mattresses covered by a cream eiderdown patterned with red roses and a frilly red border. On the key to her night table, a ribbon. On every drawer in the chest of drawers, another ribbon. And every key to every door had a ribbon.

'I can see you're very fond of ribbons and bows,' I said.

'A home without ribbons isn't a proper home.'

And she asked me if I liked selling cakes and I said I really did, yes, madam, especially curling the end of the string with the tip of the scissors and I couldn't wait for the holidays to come when I'd wrap up lots of parcels and hear the cash register and doorbell ringing all the time.

'I don't believe you,' she said.

Late in the afternoon Joe dug his elbow into me and said, 'Let's be off.'

And when we were in the doorway his mother asked me, 'And do you like housework as well?'

'Yes, madam, I really do.'

'That's just as well.'

Then she told us to wait, went back into the house and came out with some black rosary beads she gave me as a present. When we were some way away, Joe said I'd completely won her over.

'What did she say when you were alone with her in the kitchen?'

'That you were a very good lad.'

'Just what I thought she said.'

When he said that, he stared at the ground and kicked a pebble. I told him I didn't know what I'd do with the rosary beads. He told me to put them in a drawer, that they might come in useful some day. You should never throw anything away.

And he pinched me under my arm. While I was rubbing it, because he'd really hurt me, he asked me whether I could remember something or other, and then said he'd soon buy a motorbike, and that would suit us down to the ground, because when we were married, we'd ride round the whole country and I'd ride pillion. He asked me if I'd ever ridden pillion behind a boy and I said I never had, that I thought it looked very dangerous, and he looked as happy as a lark, and said, ah, love ... it's a piece of cake ...

We went to the Monumental to have a drink and eat baby octopus. He met Ernie there, and Ernie, with his big cow-like eyes and slightly twisted mouth, said he'd found a flat on Montseny, quite cheap but in a bad state because the landlord couldn't be bothered with it, and the new tenants would have to do any refurbishing. It was an attic flat and we liked the sound of it, even more so when he said the roof terrace would be all ours. It would be all ours because the ground-floor neighbours had a yard and those on the first floor had a long, steep staircase down to a small garden with a chicken coop and washhouse. Joe got very enthusiastic and told Ernie he mustn't let it out of his hands and Ernie said he'd go with Matthew the day after and we should come as well. All together. Joe asked him if he knew of any second-hand motorbikes because Ernie worked in his uncle's garage and he said he'd watch out for one. They chatted away as if I didn't exist. My mother had never told me about men. She and my father spent years and years together arguing and a good few more not saying a word. They'd spend Sunday afternoons sitting in the dining room not saying a word to each other. When my mother died, this life without words extended. And when my father remarried several years later, I had nothing at home to latch on to. I lived a cat's life, running all over, tail up, tail down, time to eat, time to sleep, except a cat doesn't have to work to survive. We lived in a house without words and I found the things that came to me frightening because I never knew what sparked them off . . .

When we all said goodbye at the tram stop, I heard Ernie say, I don't know where you got her from, she's a real find . . . And I heard Joe laugh, ha, ha, ha . . .

I put the rosary beads on the night table and went to take a look at the garden down below. Our neighbours' son, on leave from his military service, was enjoying the cool air. I screwed up a ball of paper, threw it at him and hid.

IV

'I think it's a good idea to marry young. You need a husband and a roof over your head.'

Mrs Enriqueta, who lived by selling roast chestnuts and sweet potatoes on the corner by the Smart cinema in winter and peanuts and almonds during the long summer holidays, always gave me good advice. She'd sit opposite me, when we were under the glass-fronted balcony, and she'd roll her sleeves up and down, said nothing when rolling them up, then once they were up she started talking and never stopped. She was tall, with an angler-fish mouth and an ice-cream cornet of a nose. Summer and winter, she always wore white stockings and black shoes. She was clean and tidy and very fond of her coffee. She had a painting, hanging on a piece of red and yellow string, that was full of locusts wearing gold coronets, with men's faces and women's hair, crawling out of a pit on to scorched grass, and the sea in the distance and the sky above were the colour of ox-blood and the locusts, clad in iron armour, were killing each other with swipes of their tails. It was raining outside. Drizzling on terraces, streets and gardens, and on the sea, as if the sea needed more water, and maybe on the mountains. We could hardly see them and it was early afternoon. Drops of rain played chase on the washing lines and, sometimes, one dripped down and, before it fell, it stretched and stretched because it seemed it was a huge effort to let go. It had been raining for a week, drizzle, not too heavy or too light, and the low clouds were so full of drizzle they dragged their swollen bellies along the roofs. We watched the rain.

'I think Joe will be much better for you than Pete. He's got a small business. Pete is always at someone else's beck and call. Joe's smarter and more of a go-getter.'

'But sometimes he gives a deep sigh and says, poor Mary . . . '

'But you're the one he's marrying, aren't you?'

My feet were frozen because my shoes were soaked and the top of my head felt red-hot. I told her Joe wanted to buy a motorbike and she said that showed how up-to-date he was. And Mrs Enriqueta went with me to buy the material for my bridal outfit and was very pleased when I said we might be renting a flat near hers.

It was in a terrible state. The kitchen stank of cockroaches and I found a nest of long, toffee-coloured eggs, and Joe said take a good look round because you'll find a lot more where they came from. The dining-room wallpaper was lined with little hoops. Joe said he wanted apple green, and cream in the baby's bedroom, with a frieze of clowns. And a new kitchen. He told Ernie to tell Matthew he wanted to see him. We all went to the flat on Sunday afternoon. Matthew started stripping the kitchen straight away, and a labourer, with bits all over his trousers, took the rubble out and tipped it into a barrow they'd parked in the street. But the labourer made a mess on the stairs and a first-floor neighbour came out and said we should sweep up before we left because she didn't want to slip and break a leg ... and Joe kept saying people might be stealing our barrow ... We helped Ernie wet the walls of the dining-room and scrape the paper off. After we'd been hard at it for a while we realised Joe had disappeared. Ernie said Joe wriggled away like an eel whenever he didn't want to do something. I went into the kitchen for a glass of water. The back of Matthew's shirt was sopping wet and his face shone with sweat as he hammered on the chisel. I started scraping again. And Ernie said that Joe would just laugh his absence off when he came back and he was sure it would be very late. It was hard work scraping the paper off, first one layer, then another, five altogether. It was dark and we were washing our hands when Joe finally turned up and said he'd been helping the labourer to load the rubble into the barrow when one of his customers had walked by ... Ernie said, and time just flew by, I expect ... And Joe ignored him completely and said it would be more work than he'd expected but we'd manage. When we went to go downstairs, Matthew said they'd make me a kitchen fit for a queen. And then Joe decided he wanted to go up to the roof terrace. It was breezy and you could see lots of terraces, though the first-floor flat's bay window blocked our view of the street. Then we left. The wall between our landing and the first floor was covered in chalk drawings: names and little stick men. And among the names and the stick men there was a set of scales, really well drawn, the lines scored deep into the wall as if they'd used a chisel. One of the scales was set slightly below the other. I ran my finger over the edge of one of the pans. We went to get a drink and eat baby octopus. We had another row in the middle of the week because of Joe's obsession with the pastry-cook.

'If I see him staring at your behind again, I'll go in and he'll be the worse for wear,' he shouted. He disappeared for a couple of days and when he re-emerged, I asked him if he'd got over it and he strutted like a rooster and said I'd some explaining to do because he'd seen me out with Pete. I said he must have mistaken me for another girl. He said it *was* me. I swore it wasn't and he said it was. At first I spoke quietly but as he didn't believe me I started screaming and, when he heard me, he said all girls were crazy and rubbish and I asked him where he'd seen me with Pete.

'In the street.'

'But which street?'

'In the street.'

'But which street? Which street?'

He marched off. I didn't sleep that night. He came back in the morning and said I must promise never to go out with Pete again, end all that business and he'd never lose his temper with me again, I said all right and I'd never go out with Pete again. Instead of being pleased he flew into a rage, and said he was sick of me lying, that he'd set a trap for me and caught me like a mouse, and he said I should beg for forgiveness for going for a walk with Pete and I told him I hadn't but in the end he made me believe I had and that was when he told me to get down on my knees.

'In the middle of the street?'

'Kneel down inside your head.'

And he made me beg for forgiveness down on my knees inside my head, because I'd gone for a walk with Pete who, poor soul, I hadn't seen since we'd split up. On Sunday I went to scrape wallpaper. Joe didn't come until we'd finished because he'd had to work on a piece of furniture that was on order.

Matthew had almost finished the kitchen. One more afternoon and it would be ready. White tiles to about waist height. And shiny tiles above the stove. Matthew said he'd brought all the tiles from his workplace. He said it was his wedding present. He hugged Joe, and Ernie, with those dreamy cow eyes of his, was washing his hands. We all went off for a drink and baby octopus. Ernie said if we needed a ring he knew a jeweller who'd sell us one at a good price. And Matthew said he knew one who'd sell us one for half-price.

'I don't know how you do it,' Joe replied.

And all blond and blue-eyed, Matthew laughed cheerfully and glanced from Joe to me, 'I got the skills.'

V

The night before Palm Sunday, my father asked me when we were getting married. He was on his way to the dining-room, in those shoes of his with the well-worn heels. I said we didn't know ... when the flat was ready.

'How long will that be then?'

I told him I couldn't say because it depended on how long it took. There were at least five layers of wallpaper to scrape off and Joe wanted every one removed because he wanted everything just so and to last a lifetime.

'Invite him to lunch on Sunday.'

I told Joe and he hit the roof.

'I went to ask for your hand and he tried to put me off and said I was the third and he didn't know if I'd be the last, trying to put me off even more, and now he wants to invite me to Sunday lunch? Let him wait until we're married ... '

We went to a blessing. There were boys in the street with plaited palm fronds and girls with small palm leaves and boys and girls with rattles and some wielded wooden maces instead,

21

pretending to kill Jews on walls, on the ground, on the tops of tins or an old bucket or anywhere you could think of. By the time we got to the Josepets, everyone was shouting. Matthew came with us, carrying his baby girl round his neck. She was as pretty as a little flower and he carried her as if she really was one. She had very fair curly hair and blue eyes like her father's, but was a baby girl who never laughed. She was clutching a palm frond studded with glazed cherries, which Matthew was half holding. Another father was carrying a young boy round his neck and he was clutching a small white frond with a blue silk bow and twinkling diamond star, and the crowd was pushing the two fathers, and without noticing, they got closer and closer until the boy started snatching cherries from Matthew's daughter's frond and by the time we cottoned on half the frond was missing its cherries.

We went to Joe's mother's for lunch. She'd tied lots of sprigs of box to the table with red ribbon and tied small fronds together with sky-blue ribbon. She said she did that every year to please her friends. And she gave me a sprig with a red ribbon because I said I'd blessed the palm. And a lady came in from the garden and Joe's mother introduced us. She was a neighbour Joe's mother had asked in because she'd had a row with her husband.

After we had started lunch, Joe asked for some salt. His mother looked up sharply and said she always cooked with plenty of salt. And Joe said it was tasteless today. The neighbour said she didn't think it was too salty or tasteless: it was just right. And Joe said it couldn't have been more tasteless. His mother got up very stiffly, went into the kitchen and returned with a rabbit-shaped salt cellar. The salt came out of the rabbit's ears. She put the salt cellar on the table, and snapped, salt. And rather than putting salt on his plate, Joe started saying we were all salty ever since that lady who'd doubted her husband had suddenly swung round when he'd asked her to walk straight on. Joe's mother told him to be quiet and eat and he asked their neighbour if he was right or not to say she shouldn't have turned round, and the neighbour chewed and swallowed politely, and said she didn't have a clue what he was talking about.

And Joe then said what the hell, and once he'd said that, he shut up and shook salt all over his plate and then told his mother, look, can't you see, not a speck of salt. You spent the morning making bows and didn't add a speck of salt. I sided with his mother and said she *had* put some salt in the food. And the neighbour said she couldn't stand food that was too salty and Joe said now he got what had happened, his mother hadn't added any salt to please *her*, but it was one thing to cook lunch to please a neighbour and quite another to try to make her son believe she'd added salt. And he kept shaking salt over his plate and his mother crossed herself and when Joe had decided that he'd added enough he put the cellar back on the table and started talking about salt again. And how everyone knew that the devil ... And his mother told him not to keep harping on like that, but he did all the same, and said that the devil had created diabetics, who were made of sugar, just to annoy us. We are all salt, sweat and tears ... and he told me, lick your hand and see what it tastes like. And it was the devil again and the neighbour said I reckon you're still a little kid who believes in the devil, and Joe said it was the devil again, and his mother told him to shut up. And Joe still hadn't eaten a bite and we were halfway through our food and that was when he said the devil was God's shadow and that he too was everywhere, in plants, on mountains, outside, in the street, and inside houses, above and below ground, and that he buzzed around disguised as a big black bluebottle, with red and blue juices, and when he was a bluebottle, he gorged on rubbish and half-rotten dead animals that had been dumped on the tip. And he took his plate away and said he wasn't hungry and would only eat the pudding.

The next Sunday he came for lunch at my house and gave my father a gift of a cigar. I'd brought a long cream roll. Joe talked about wood for the whole meal and about how some woods lasted longer than others. While we were drinking our coffee, Joe asked me if I wanted to leave early or preferred to stay on. I told him I wasn't worried either way. But my father's wife said it was better for young folk to go and enjoy themselves, so we were soon walking down the street under a blistering sun at three in the afternoon. We went to the flat to scrape paper. We found Ernie there who'd brought two rolls of wallpaper and was looking at them with Matthew and he said he knew a decorator who'd paper everything for free if Joe gave him legs for a table he had with very worm-eaten legs that was half falling apart because when his kids were by themselves at home they banged it on the floor and tried to make it fall apart completely. And they agreed that this was a good idea.

And when the dining-room was papered, a big damp patch appeared down the right hand side. They told the lad who'd done the papering to come back and he said that he wasn't to blame, and the patch must have appeared later. That the wall was to blame and a pipe must have burst inside. And Joe said the patch had been there all the time and he should have said there was a damp problem. Matthew said we'd better go and see the neighbours because they probably had a leaky sink on their side and if they had there wasn't much we could do. The three of them went next door and the people were very rude; we might have a damp patch but they didn't and they gave us their landlord's address. The landlord said he'd send someone to look at the damp but nobody came, and finally he came in person and said it was a problem we, or our landlord, would have to pay for because we'd caused it when we'd used a drill. Joe said we hadn't used a drill. The landlord said it came from all that banging when we installed the kitchen and he was washing his hands of the whole business. Joe went crazy. Matthew said if something had to be repaired the best would be to split it fifty-fifty. But the neighbours' landlord didn't want to know, you talk to your own landlord . . . he retorted.

'If the damp's coming through from your side, why the hell should we talk to our landlord?' And the landlord said even if it came from his side he could prove there was nothing on his side causing a damp patch. He left and they were all arguing. And all that bother and bad words and getting angry, for nothing, for something that wasn't worth a candle, for something that disappeared the minute we put the sideboard in front of it.

We went to the Monumental every Sunday for a drink and baby octopus. One day a man in a yellow shirt came over and tried to sell us postcards of an artiste who'd been the toast of Paris years ago. He said he was her agent, and the artiste, who'd been the love of princes and kings, lived by herself now and was selling off her belongings and her souvenirs. Joe screamed at him and sent him packing. When we left he said I could go home now because he had to see a gentleman who wanted him to refurbish three bedrooms. I went for a little window-shopping on the High Street. And for a look at the dolls in the emporium window. A few idiots started saying things to annoy me and one who looked like a gypsy came closer than most and said, she's

25

tasty. As if I were a bowl of soup. I wasn't at all amused. However, it was true my father always said I was a prickly so-and-so . . . On the other hand, I really did feel that I didn't know what I was doing on this planet.

VI

He said he'd take me to see Father John. And while we were about it, that we'd have to pay the rent for the flat between us. As if we were friends. That led to bawling and shouting at home because my father looked after the little I had left after his wife had taken out her slice for the food I ate. In the end my father said he would pay half the rent. But Joe had only mentioned the business of the rent when we were on our way to see Father John.

Father John looked as if he was made from the wings of a fly, I mean his clothes did. That kind of watery black. He greeted us like a saint. Joe said, the wedding should be over and done with in a flash, as far as I'm concerned, and the cheaper the better, and if it can be over in five minutes rather than ten, I'll be happy. Father John, who'd known Joe since he was a child, splayed his hands over his knees and, bleary-eyed, because you could see age had affected his eyes, said, not likely, marriage is for life and is very, very important. Don't you put on your very best clothes on a Sunday? Well, marriage starts like a special

Sunday and requires lots of ceremony. If we don't respect such an act we'll be behaving in a most uncivilised ... And I think you'd rather be civilised, wouldn't you? Joe stared at the ground as he listened, and when he was about to say something Father John gestured to him not to.

'I *will* marry you and I think it would be best to take it calmly. I know you young people are full of energy and keen to get on with life, and live in a rush, but life, I mean proper life, should not be lived in a hurry ... I think your fiancée would prefer to wear a wedding dress so everyone who sees her knows she is a bride, and not wear an everyday kind of dress, even if it is a new one ... Girls are like that. And all the marriages I have blessed ... all the good ones, that is to say, had brides who dressed as brides.'

When we left, Joe said, 'I've a lot of respect for him because he is such a good man.'

The brass bedstead was the only thing I took from my house; it was the only thing that was mine. Ernie gave us a wrought-iron lamp for the dining-room. It came with strawberry-coloured tassels and hung from the ceiling on three iron chains set in a three-petal metal flower. I wore a bridal dress with a long train. Joe wore a dark suit. The apprentice and Ernie's family also came: three sisters and two married brothers with their wives. My father led me to the altar. Joe's mother wore a black silk dress that rustled whenever she moved, and Julie, a dress of fine ash-grey lace with a pink bow. We were a merry band. Matthew's wife, who was called Griselda, couldn't come at the last minute because she didn't feel well and Matthew said it often happened and we should excuse her. It all went on and on and Father John gave a lovely sermon. He talked about Adam and Eve, the apple and the snake, and said woman was made from a man's rib and that Adam found her sleeping next to him and Our Lord hadn't prepared him for such a big surprise. He told us what Paradise was like: rippling brooks and freshly mown meadows and sky-blue flowers, and the first thing Eve did when she woke up was to pick a blue flower and blow on it and a few petals flew through the air and Adam scolded her because she'd hurt a flower. Because Adam, who was the father of all men, only wanted what was good. And everything ended with the fiery sword ... Like the morning dew, said Mrs Enriqueta who was sitting behind me, and I wondered what Father John would say if he ever saw her painting of the locusts with the crazy faces who killed with their tails ... Everybody said it was one of the loveliest sermons Father John had ever given and the apprentice told Joe's mother that when his sister got married, Father John had also talked about Paradise and the first mother and father, the angel and the flaming sword ... exactly the same; only the flowers were different, he'd said they were yellow when his sister got married, and he'd said the water in the brooks was blue in the morning and pink in the afternoon.

We went to the vestry to sign the forms and then cars took us to Montjuïc, so we could walk up an appetite. And when we'd been for a stroll, while our guests had a drink, Joe and I went to have our photos taken. The photographer took shots of Joe standing up and me sitting down and Joe sitting down and me standing up. And both of us sitting down with our backs half turned and another with us sitting and looking at each other, so it doesn't look as if you're always arguing, joked the photographer. And another standing side by side, me with a hand on a wobbly, three-legged table, and one of us sitting on a bench, next to a tree made of tulle and paper. By the time we got to the Monumental, people said they'd got tired of waiting for us and we retorted that the photographer had taken lots of artistic photos and that needed time. The fact was that all the olives and anchovies had disappeared and Joe said he didn't mind and we should start lunch, but then he said they were a bunch of rude so-and-so's. And he argued with Ernie the whole lunch ... about the olives, whatever happened to the olives, and Matthew said nothing, he simply looked at me, and laughed now and then. And he leaned across behind my father's chair and said, they always make me laugh. We ate a delicious lunch and then they played records and we all started dancing. My father danced with me. I danced in my veil, and in the end took it off and gave it to Mrs Enriqueta so it didn't get in my way. And when I danced, I gathered up my dress because I was afraid people would tread on my train and I waltzed and Matthew waltzed beautifully and led me lightly as a feather, as if my whole life had been one long waltz, he led me so beautifully. My cheeks were ablaze. I danced with the apprentice who hardly knew how and Joe cracked a joke trying to annoy him but the apprentice carried on and ignored him. And four gentlemen came in halfway through the dance, who'd been having lunch in the room next door, and asked if we'd let them join in. They were all getting on, some well into their forties. The four were soon joined by two more. Half a dozen all told. And they said they were celebrating an appendicitis operation the youngster had just had, the fellow with a deaf-aid dangling from his ear because he was hard of hearing. It had been a great success, as we could see, and when they'd heard there was a wedding party next door they'd decided to ask to join in the dance because they wanted to feel young and happy again. And all those gentlemen congratulated me and asked me who the lucky man was and gave him cigars and they all danced with me and it was one long laugh, and when he saw that the gents celebrating the operation had joined us, the waiter serving the liqueurs asked if he could dance with the bride, because it was a special tradition of his and brought good luck. He said if we didn't mind he'd write my name down in a notebook where he'd recorded the names of all the brides he'd ever danced with and he did just that, and showed us the book with seven pages full of names. He was like a beanpole, with sunken cheeks and just one tooth, and wore his hair all combed over to one side to hide his bald patch. When I was about to dance with the waiter, who wanted, he said, to dance a waltz, Joe put on a lively *paso doble* and the waiter and I shot up and down like a couple of darts and everybody was very happy and halfway through Joe said he wanted to finish the *paso doble* with me because he'd met me dancing a *paso doble*, and the waiter handed me over to Joe and then ran his hand over his head to flatten his hair, but it escaped him and flew all over the place. The old gentlemen stood in a line by the door, dressed in black with white carnations in their buttonholes, and as I danced I could see them out of the corner of my eye and they looked as if they'd just arrived from another planet. While we danced, Joe said they'd tried to make a fool of him, because all we needed now was Father John and his sermon to come and poop the party. Everybody clapped and I was breathless and my heart was thumping and I was so happy my eyes sparkled. And when it all ended, I wanted it to be yesterday again, so we could start all over again, it was so wonderful ...

VII

We'd been married for two months and one week. Joe's mother had given us a mattress and Mrs Enriqueta an old eiderdown with crocheted flowers that bulged out. The mattress cover was blue with a bright, curly feather pattern. The bed was a light-coloured wood. The head and posts were made of rows of little columns and the columns were made of little balls aligned one on top of another. There was more than enough room for a person to hide under the bed. I found that out for myself the day I first wore the chestnut-brown dress with the smart cream collar that I'd made myself. The skirt was pleated with small gilt buttons down the front. After dinner, while Joe was designing a piece of furniture on the table in the circle of light from the lamp, I thought I'd give him a surprise and walked into the dining-room in my new dress without saying a word. Joe didn't look up, but just asked: 'So what were you being so quiet about?'

He looked at me and the shadow from the strawberry tassels fell over one side of his face and days ago we'd said we'll hang the lamp higher up so it gives more light. I stood opposite him and he stared and didn't say a word and stayed like that for a good while until I couldn't stand it any more, and he simply kept staring. In the half-dark, his eyes seemed even smaller and more sunken and when I thought I couldn't stand it any more, he shot up like a jet of water, splayed his hands in the air as if the skin between his fingers was about to split, and chased after me shouting wooh wooh wooh wooh ... wooh wooh wooh wooh ... I dashed down the passage with Joe in hot pursuit, wooh wooh wooh wooh ... wooh wooh wooh wooh ... I ran into our bedroom and he came after me and shoved me on to the floor and kicked me under the bed and jumped on top of the bed. When I tried to come out he slapped the top of my head and shouted: 'Naughty girl!' And whichever side I tried to come out on, *slap!* down came his hand: 'Naughty girl!' Afterwards he played that same trick on me lots of times.

One day I spotted some lovely hot chocolate cups and bought six: they were white and heavy. The second Joe saw them he lost his temper: why on earth do we need six hot chocolate cups?

Then Ernie came and didn't even bother to ask how we were, he said Matthew had a friend who knew a gentleman who lived on carrer Bertran and he wanted to restore all the furniture in his house. He says you should go tomorrow at one. The house is on three floors. You can recoup all you spent on the wedding, and this fellow is in a hurry and he'll have to pay you overtime. Joe jotted down the address and opened the kitchen cupboard, look what we're wasting our time on now ... Neither of us likes hot chocolate. She just does the first thing that comes into her head ... Ernie picked up a cup, laughed and pretended to drink from it, then put it back next to the others. It was made plain that I didn't like hot chocolate.

Joe bought himself a second-hand motorbike with the money he earned restoring the furniture of the gentleman who lived on carrer Bertran. He bought a bike that had belonged to a man who had died in an accident. They'd only found his corpse the day after. We whistled along the roads and through villages on that bike frightening poultry and putting the fear of God into people.

'Hang on tight, we're going to break records now.'

I hated it most when we went round corners. We screeched round almost level with the ground and, on the straight, we'd pick up. 'When you met me you never thought I'd make you a speed merchant, did you?' When we swerved round bends, my face froze and went as stiff as a board, my eyes streamed and I pressed my cheek against Joe's back and the whole journey I'd think I'd never see home again.

'We'll do the coast road today.'

We ate lunch in Badalona and didn't get any further because we'd got up too late. The sea didn't look at all like water and was sad and dismal under the overcast sky. And the fish breathing below churned up the waves and their fishy bad temper made the sea surge and foam. When we were drinking our coffee, that vicious stab in the back once again, poor Mary . . .

I couldn't stop the blood pouring from my nose. I put a ten-cent coin between my eyebrows and our huge front-door key down the back of my neck. The waiter in the café accompanied me to the lavatory and helped me douse my head in water. When I came back, Joe was pursing his lips and his nose had gone bright red in rage, I'll get my own back with the tip. He won't get a cent.

He said the waiter shouldn't have gone with me and I asked him why *he* hadn't and he said I was big enough to look after myself. When he got back on the bike, more of the usual, if only Mary could see this hundred c.c. . . .

I began to take it seriously. Several days before he'd say poor Mary, I knew exactly when it was coming because he went limp. And when he'd said poor Mary and could see I was upset, he'd go all still as if I wasn't there, but I felt he was less agitated. And I couldn't get poor Mary out of my head. If I swept the floor, I'd think, Mary must do this better than me. If I washed the dishes, I'd think, Mary must wash them cleaner. If I made the bed, I'd think, Mary must leave the sheets smoother . . . And Mary was all I could think, endlessly . . . I hid the hot chocolate cups. When I thought how I'd bought them without first asking for Joe's permission, my heart shrank. And Joe's mother, the moment she saw me, what, no news yet?

And Joe dangled his arms by his sides, showed her the palms of his hands, shrugged his shoulders and said nothing. But I could hear the words he was choking down and those words were, it's not my fault. And his mother stared at me and her eyes would glaze over, perhaps she's not getting enough to eat . . . She'd touch my arms, she's not so skinny . . .

'She likes to play tricks,' Joe said, staring at us both. When we went to his mother's, she always said she'd cooked us a million-dollar lunch. And when we left, Joe always asked, what do you think of my mother's cooking? And we got on the motorbike. Brrmbrrmbrrm . . . brrmbrrmbrrm . . . Thunder and lightning. At night, when I was undressing, you up for it? Today's Sunday and we're going to make a kid. The next morning he'd shoot out of bed throwing the bedclothes in the air, not looking to see whether he'd left me any. Straight to the balcony to take deep breaths. He washed, making a din, and sang as he walked into the dining-room. He sat down and wrapped his legs around the legs of his chair. I still hadn't been to his shop and one day he said I should. The glass door had flaking paint and dusty panes of glass you couldn't see in or out of. When I said I'd clean them, he said, you leave my shop alone. The tools looked lovely and he had two pots of glue, one with glue that had dripped over the side and dried, and he slapped my hand when I touched the stick in the pot, hey, keep off!

And he introduced me to his apprentice as if we hadn't already met, Pidgey, my wife. The apprentice with his scheming face held out a hand as if he were offering me a dead branch. Andy, if I can be of any help ...

And it was always the same story. Pidgey, Pidgey ... And his mother, what, no news yet? And the day when I said the plates piled high made me feel sick and couldn't she put less on for me, Joe's mother said, and about time too! She made me go into her bedroom. There were bows on the four posts of her black bed with the red-rose eiderdown: blue, lilac, yellow and carrot-coloured. She made me lie down, touched me and listened close to my body like a doctor; not yet, she said, as she went back into the dining-room. And Joe knocked his cigar ash on the floor and said he could have told her so.

VIII

And he made the chair. Night after night he'd pore over his plans, then come to bed when I was already snoozing. He'd wake me up to tell me the most difficult bit was making it balance. He'd discuss his design with Ernie and Matthew when we spent Sundays at home because the weather was so bad. It was very strange: part ordinary, part rocking chair, part armchair, and he took ages to make it. He told me it was Majorcan. All wood. It rocked very little. And he said I ought to make a cushion the same colour as the lampshade. Two: one for him to sit on and one to rest his head on. Only *he* was allowed to sit in that chair.

'It's a man's chair,' he said. I didn't go near it. He said you should polish it every Saturday to bring out the grain and make it gleam. He sat in the chair and crossed his legs. If he was smoking, he'd half shut his eyes as if he were in seventh heaven, and exhale. I told Mrs Enriqueta about all that.

'He's not hurting anyone, is he? He's better finding his fun sitting in that chair than riding his motorbike like a lunatic.'

And she told me to take care with Joe's mother, and above all, not to let *him* guess whatever I was thinking, because he was one who liked upsetting people and better not to let on about my weak points. I told her I quite liked Joe's mother because she had that comic habit of making bows. But Mrs Enriqueta said she'd thought about her bows and it was her way of duping people into thinking she was an innocent soul. But yes, right, I should make it plain that I liked her, because Joe would be pleased with me if his mother liked me.

On the Sundays when we didn't go out because it was raining and Ernie and Matthew didn't come, we'd spend the afternoon in the bed with the honey-coloured columns made from those wooden balls. And when we were having lunch, he'd declare, 'We'll make a baby today.'

And he made me see stars. Mrs Enriqueta had been dropping heavy hints for some time about really wanting to know what my wedding night had been like. But I didn't dare because we didn't have a wedding night. We had a wedding week. Up to that point when he was taking his clothes off, you could say I'd never really taken a proper look at him. I sat in a corner of the room, not daring to move, and in the end he said, if you're embarrassed to take your clothes off in front of me I'll go out, and if not, I'll start and then you'll see it's not such a big deal. He had a forest of hair over his round head that shone like patent leather. He combed and then flattened it with his other hand after he'd done with the comb. When he didn't have a comb he splayed his fingers wide, and one hand chased the other over his head. When he didn't comb his hair, a fringe fell over his broad, low forehead. His bushy, black eyebrows arched above his beady, shining mouse eyes. The sides of his eyes were always damp, as if he'd greased them lightly, and that made him look lovely. His nose wasn't too broad or too narrow or turned up, which I would have hated. His cheeks were full, pinkish in summer and red in winter, and one of his ears jutted slightly out at the side of his head. His lips were always red and fleshy and his lower lip stuck out a bit. When he was talking or laughing, you could see his two rows of teeth, with each tooth snuggling in his gums. His neck was soft and smooth. And his nose, as I've said, wasn't too broad or narrow and each nostril was home to a tuft of hair that kept out the cold and the dust. The veins on the back of his quite skinny legs sometimes stood out like snakes. His whole body was long and round in the right places. His chest was high and his buttocks tight. His feet were long and thin, with slightly fallen arches that meant his heels collided when he wasn't wearing shoes. He was well built and when I told him that, he turned slowly round and said, do you really think so?

I was terrified in my little corner. And when he got into bed, after setting me an example, as he'd said, I started taking my clothes off. I'd always been afraid of that moment. People had told me it's a path of roses getting that far and a path of tears from then on. And they make you happy just to disappoint . . . Because from my childhood I'd heard people say they split you open. And I'd always been really afraid of being split open and dying. Women, people would say, die split asunder . . . You start to suffer the day you marry. And if you're not properly split open, the midwife will complete the job with a knife or a bit of broken bottle and then you stay like that for ever, gutted or sewn up, and that's why married women get tired so quickly if they have to stand up for any length of time. And that's why gentlemen who are in the know stand up when the tram is packed and women are standing, and insist they sit down, and gentlemen who aren't remain seated. And when I started to cry, Joe lifted his head above the turn of the blanket and asked what was wrong and I told him the truth, I was afraid of being split open and dying. And he laughed and said he'd certainly heard of a case, Queen Bustamante, whose husband had a horse split her open to save himself the bother and she died. And Joe laughed himself silly. That was why I couldn't tell Mrs Enriqueta about my wedding night, because the day we went to live in our flat, Joe sent me off to get supplies in, and then locked and bolted the door and we had a week of wedding nights. All the same I told Mrs Enriqueta about the case of Queen Bustamante and she said yes, that was horrific, but what *her* husband did to her was even more horrific, that husband the rain had been watering for years ever since he'd kicked the bucket. He'd tied her to their bed as if she'd been crucified because she was always trying to run away. And when she started insisting I told her about my wedding night, I tried to distract her, and one good way to do that was to recount the saga of the rocking chair. And the story of the lost key.

IX

One night we went walking with Ernie until two a.m. after we'd done at the Monumental. And when we were in front of our house and Ernie was about to go, we found we couldn't get in. Our front-door key had disappeared. Joe said he'd given it to me to keep in my purse. Ernie had had dinner with us, and he said he thought he remembered seeing Joe take it from its hook behind the door, where we always kept it, and put it in his pocket. Joe turned all his pockets out in case he had a hole somewhere. I said perhaps he'd dreamed I'd taken it. Joe said perhaps he'd told Ernie to take the key and Ernie had done so without thinking and didn't remember and he was the one who'd lost it. Then they both said I was the one who'd taken it but they didn't remember when and neither had seen me do it. Ernie said, ring the first-floor flat. Joe didn't want to and he was right. It was better not to involve our first-floor neighbours. And finally Joe said, lucky we've got the shop, let's go and get some tools.

They went to get tools to open the door. I stayed by the

entrance in case the nightwatchman turned up, because I'd clapped my hands on the street corner but he hadn't come and was nowhere to be seen. I soon tired of being on my feet and sat down on the step. I leaned my head against the door and looked up at the scrap of sky between the houses. There was a light breeze and dark clouds were scudding across the very dark sky. I found it a strain to keep my eyes open. I was fighting off sleep. And the pitch dark, the breeze and the clouds chasing in the same direction were making me drowsy, and I worried about what Joe and Ernie would say if they found me curled up asleep when they came back, and so soundly asleep I couldn't go upstairs ... I heard their footsteps in the distance, over the cobblestones.

Joe drilled a hole above the keyhole. Ernie kept saying it wasn't legal and Joe kept saying he'd fill the hole in but first he had to get into his own house. And when he'd drilled the hole through the door, he made a hook from a piece of wire and fished out the string – the string you had to pull to open the door from the inside – and managed to open it just as the night-watchman walked round the corner. We went in quickly and Ernie made himself scarce. When we walked into our flat, the first thing we saw was the key hanging up behind the door. The day after, Joe plugged the hole with a cork, and if anyone had noticed, they never said anything. So after all that, you hadn't lost the key, said Mrs Enriqueta. I replied, as long as we thought we'd lost it, it was as if we really had.

And the time had come round for the big street party. Joe said we'd dance in Diamond Square and dance the lucky posy dance ... We spent the fiesta days shut up at home and Joe was in a bad temper because he'd done some restoring that had been a lot of work and the gentleman he'd done it for turned out to be a Jew and had diddled him and to put it behind him Joe had settled, but he'd lost money over it. And his rage turned on me. And when he was in a rage, he'd say, Pidgey, watch out, Pidgey, you've made a mess, come here, Pidgey, clear off, Pidgey. You are so calm and collected ... And he'd stalk from one side to the other like a caged beast. And he'd start opening all the drawers and throwing the contents on the floor and when I asked him what he was looking for he'd not reply. He was furious with me because I wasn't furious with the man who'd diddled him. And as I refused to be furious, I left him to his own devices. I combed my hair and when I opened the door to go out and told him I was going out to get a drink because all the mess he'd made had given me a thirst, he stopped acting crazy. The whole street looked happy and cheerful and pretty girls were walking up and down in their party dresses and a shower of bright-coloured confetti fell on me from a balcony and I poked some pieces into my hair so they would stay put. I brought two bottles home and Joe was sitting on his chair half asleep. The streets looked happy and cheerful while I picked clothes up off the floor, folded them and put them away. And later on we motorbiked over to his mother to say hello.

'Are you enjoying life together?'

'Yes, madam.'

As soon as we'd left her place and Joe was kicking the bike off, he asked, what were you two whispering about?

I said I'd told his mother he had a lot of work on and he retorted that that wasn't a good thing to say because his mother was a big spender and she'd been wanting him to buy her a broom for cobwebs for some time, not to mention a new white and grey mattress cover. And one day Joe's mother told me that

43

he was stubborn and, when he was a young kid, he used to drive her mad. When she told him to do something and he didn't want to, he just sat on the ground and wouldn't get up until she belted him round the head.

And it was a Sunday morning when Joe started complaining about his leg. He said his leg hurt him when he was asleep, as if the marrow in his bones was on fire, or sometimes as if the fire was between his bone and his flesh. And the fire wasn't always in his bone marrow, but when it was he never felt it between his flesh and his bones. The moment I put my feet on the ground, it stops.

'Which bone?'

'Which bones, you mean! The bone in my calf a bit and my thigh bone, but my knee is fine.' He said it might be rheumatism. Mrs Enriqueta said she didn't believe a word; he was only doing that so I would look after him. He complained about his leg for the whole winter. And every morning, when he was opening his eyes, and in the middle of breakfast, he'd tell me in minute detail how his leg had hurt that night. His mother said, Pidgey should give you hot towels. And he said he didn't want that bother, all that pain was bad enough. As soon as I saw him come in, whether it was midday or midnight, I'd ask after his leg, and he said most days it didn't hurt.

He lay on his bed. He'd drop down like a sack and I was always on tenterhooks thinking he'd break the springs. He wanted me to take his shoes off and put on his light brown plaid slippers. After resting for a while he'd come and eat his dinner. Before going to sleep he wanted me to rub spirit all over his body, to help against the pain, he said. And it had to be his whole body, he said, because pain was a slippery customer and would flit up or down if I left areas unrubbed.

I told everyone he only had pain at night and everyone said it was very odd. And the grocer's wife from downstairs thought it was odd too. Does his leg still keep him awake? And, what about your husband's leg? Fine, thank you very much. It only hurts at night. Is his leg still hurting? his mother asked.

One day, at the flower stalls on the Rambla, standing before a riot of smells and colours, I heard a voice behind me ...

'Natalia ...'

I didn't think anyone was speaking to me, I was so used to being called Pidgey, Pidgey. It was Pete, my old fiancé. The fiancé I'd dropped. I didn't dare ask whether he'd married or was courting. We shook hands and his lower lip trembled for a moment. He said he'd been left alone in the world. Only then did I notice he was wearing a black armband. And he looked at me as if he were about to be swallowed up among the people, among the flowers and the shops. He told me he'd met Julie one day and she'd told him I'd got married and as soon as she'd said that he'd thought how he wished me lots of luck. I looked down because I didn't know what to do or say and thought I should rein my sadness in, keep it small, not let it sur-round me, or spread to my bloodstream or thereabouts. Turn it into a little ball, bullet or pellet. Swallow it quick. And as he was quite a lot taller than me, while I was standing there with my head drooping, I felt all the pain Pete was carrying inside seep into my hair and it was as if he could see right inside me, see all my things and my sorrow. Luckily there were all those flowers.

At midday, as soon as Joe came in, the first thing I told him was that I'd met Pete.

'Pete ... ?' and he did something with his mouth. 'I don't know who you mean.'

45

'That boy I dropped so I could marry you.'

'You didn't speak to him.'

I told him we'd asked after each other, and he said I should have ignored him. And I said Pete had barely recognised me, and he'd had to look my way several times before saying hello, because I'd got so thin.

'He should mind his own business.'

And I didn't tell him that when I got off the tram I went to look at the dolls in the emporium and that was why lunch was so late.

X

Joe's mother made the sign of the cross over my forehead and wouldn't let me dry up. Well, I *was*, at last. As soon as the washing up was done she shut the kitchen door and we sat on the veranda under the grapevine on one side and Star of Bethlehem on the other, and Joe said he was tired and left us to it. That was when Joe's mother told me what Joe and Ernie had done to her one Thursday afternoon when they were kids, when Ernie always spent the afternoon with them. She said she'd planted hyacinths, some three dozen, and each morning the first thing she did when she got up was to go and see how much they'd grown. She said hyacinths grew very slowly out of their bulbs, to make you long for them, and at last little buds were parading up the stems. And you could guess from the buds what colour the flowers would be. Pink more often than not. And one Thursday the boys were playing in the garden and when she took them their mid-afternoon snack, she saw straight away that all the hyacinths had been turned upside down: the bulbs and their straggling roots above ground and the buds, leaves and stem stuck under the earth. She said she only said one word, even though she wasn't the kind to use strong language. And she refused to say which word she'd used. And she said: 'Boys give you a lot of grief. Watch it, if you have a boy.'

When my father found out I was that way – Joe went over to tell him – he came to see me and said, whether it was a boy or a girl, his name was done for.

Mrs Enriqueta was always asking me if I'd felt any sudden desires. 'If you do don't touch yourself and, if you have to, touch your behind.'

She told me about the really nasty things people crave: raisins, cherries, liver . . . The worst of all was sheep's head. She had known a lady who'd craved sheep's head. And, Mrs Enriqueta had spotted this craving later on the baby's cheek, miniature shadows of the sheep's eye and ear. And then she said babies were formed in water, first the heart, then the nerves and veins very slowly and finally the little round bones. And she said the bones in the spine were like coiled gristle, because if not they'd never fit. If wombs were longer, babies would grow straight and spines would be as stiff as a broom handle. And we wouldn't be able to bend over even when we were small.

In the summer the midwife said I needed lots of fresh air and swims in the sea. On the motorbike and off to the beach! We took food and clothes all ready. A yellow, blue and black striped towel did as a curtain. Joe held it up behind me so I could take my clothes off. He laughed at me, because I was laughable with that belly that seemed as if it didn't belong to me. I watched the waves coming and going, always the same, the same . . . all in a rush to come and go. Sat looking out at the sea that was some-times grey, sometimes green, blue more than anything else, that expanse of moving, living water, water that talked, my thoughts drained away and I was left empty. And when Joe saw I was silent for too long he'd ask, what's up with you?

I almost threw in the towel when we zigzagged back along the road when, oh poor me, my spirit shuddered and my heart was in my mouth. And Joe said that the kid was getting so used to the bike as he grew that he'd win races when he was big, he doesn't know he's riding on a bike but he can feel it and that will stick in his memory. And once we met somebody or other, I could have died there and then I was so embarrassed, because he said: she's fit to burst.

His mother kept giving me vests from when Joe was a kid and Mrs Enriqueta gave me bandages for the belly button, which was something I didn't understand. The vests had ribbons twisted through piping in the collar. They looked just right for a doll. My father said that, as his name was done for, he wanted the child to be called Louis if he were a boy, and Margaret if she were a girl, after the maternal great-grandmother. Joe said that, father-in-law or not, he would choose the name for his own child. At night when he eventually came to bed, because he was always drawing up plans on our table until late, he'd switch the light on if I was asleep and do everything he could to wake me up.

'Can you hear him now?'

And when Ernie and Matthew came, he'd say, he'll be a champion little boy!

I couldn't think what on earth I looked like, a little round ball, with feet underneath and a head on top. One Sunday Joe's mother showed me something very strange, like a dried-out root that was all flat, and she said it was a rose of Jericho she'd kept from when she'd had Joe, and when the time came, she'd put it in water and when the rose of Jericho opened, I would too.

And I got a mania for cleaning. I'd always been one for cleaning, but it got to be a real mania. I swept and dusted every day and no sooner had I finished than I began again. I spent hours polishing a tap and when I saw a mark, I'd start all over again and I loved it when it gleamed brightly. Joe wanted me to iron his trousers every week. I'd never ironed trousers before and the first time I didn't know how. I gave them a double crease behind, halfway up, even though I'd been very careful. I slept badly and everything upset me. When I woke up, I opened my hands in front of my eyes and waved them to make sure they were mine and I was still me! When I got up, my bones ached. And Joe started complaining about his leg and got into a rage. Mrs Enriqueta said Joe's illness was caused by tuberculosis of the bones and he needed sulphur. And when I told Joe, he said he wasn't going to explode just to please Mrs Enriqueta. And when I prepared him a spoonful of honey mixed with flower of sulphur, he said the honey would give him toothache all day, and he kept going on about that teeth nightmare of his: he'd been touching them one by one with the tip of his tongue and, whenever he touched one, the tooth came away from the gum and rattled in his mouth like a pebble. And his mouth filled up with pebbles that he couldn't spit out because his lips were stitched together. And after this nightmare his teeth always seemed to be on the dance and it was a dream predicting he was going to die. The grocer's wife downstairs said I should make him rinse his mouth out with poppy water, because poppy puts you to sleep and poppy water might put his pain to sleep as well, though it would wake up later, but Mrs Enriqueta said it might work but what Joe needs are a good dentist's tweezers, and that would put an end to his nightmare.

And while we were tackling his teeth, the pebbles and his

dream of death, I had an attack of nettle rash that drove me crazy. In the evening we went for a stroll to the gardens at the end of the High Street because I needed the exercise. My hands swelled, my ankles swelled, and if they'd roped me to my bed, one push would have been enough to float me. On the terrace, with breeze and the blue sky all around me, hanging out the washing or sitting down and sewing or pottering here and there, I felt as if I'd been drained empty again and was being pumped back up by something very peculiar. A mysterious person, who was well hidden, was having fun puffing into my mouth and blowing me up. Sitting on the terrace, alone in the afternoon, surrounded by the railings, the breeze and the blue sky, while I gazed at my feet totally bewildered, I let out my first cry.

XI

And that first scream of mine was deafening. Who'd have thought my voice could carry so far or last so long? Or that the pain would come out in cries from my mouth, and from the baby deeper down? Joe paced up and down the passage saying Our Fathers one after another. And once when the midwife went for some hot water she tore a strip off him, I could have well done without ...

His mother came in whenever she saw I had a moment's respite, if you could only see how Joe is suffering ... The midwife threaded a towel round the bed columns and told me to hold each end tight to help me make every effort to push hard. And when it was almost over, one column snapped and I heard a voice say, and I was so far gone I couldn't be sure whose it was, she almost strangled him.

As soon as I could breathe I heard crying and the midwife was holding a baby up by its feet like a little animal, mine now, and slapping its back, and the rose of Jericho had bloomed on the night table. I ran a hand across a flower on the crocheted eiderdown as if I was dreaming and rumpled a petal. And they said it wasn't over, the baby needed to feel mothered. And they wouldn't let me sleep, though my eyes kept closing ... I couldn't even suckle him. One of my breasts was small and flat as usual and the other was full of milk. Joe said he'd been expecting me to play some kind of joke on them. The baby boy, because it *was* a boy, weighed almost four kilos at birth and two and a half kilos a month later. He's melting away, Joe would say. He was melting like a sugar cube in a glass of water. When he's down to half a kilo, he'll die on us, now we've got him ...

Mrs Enriqueta had already heard the whole story from the grocer's wife downstairs the first time she came to see him. She says you almost strangled him? Joe was very fed up and grumbling, because of the work I'd given him, I've got to make a new column, because the way you broke it, it can't just be glued back. The baby cried at night. As soon as it was dark he'd start crying. Joe's mother said he was crying because he was afraid of the dark and Joe said the baby couldn't tell the difference between night and day. Nothing shut him up, his dummy, the bottle he wouldn't suck, being walked up and down, sung to or shouted at. Joe finally lost his patience and temper. And said that life wasn't worth living and it couldn't go on like that much longer because if it did he'd be the one who'd die. He stuck baby and cradle in a small room next to the dining-room and when we went to bed we shut the door. Our downstairs neighbours must have heard the baby crying and they started gossiping about us being bad parents. I gave him milk and he rejected it. I gave him water and he rejected it. I gave him orange juice and he spat it out. I changed him, more tears. I gave him a bath, more tears. He was restless. Always restless. And was turning into a little monkey with stick-like legs. He cried more loudly when he was naked than when he was clothed, and he wriggled his fingers as much as his toes and I was afraid he'd burst. Or that his belly button would burst open. Because his cord hadn't fallen off yet, and it should have, people said. The first day I saw him the way I'd made him, the midwife showed me how to hold him to give him a bath as she lowered him into the wash bowl: 'Before we're born we are all like pears, we've all hung from a cord like this.'

And she showed me how to lift him out of his cradle because she said if you didn't support his head, when his bones were so thin, his neck might break. And she kept telling me that the belly button was the most important part of a person. As important as the soft spot in the middle of the head when it still hadn't grown together. And the baby got more wrinkled by the day. And the skinnier he got, the louder he bawled. It was quite clear my baby had had enough of life. Julie came to visit and brought me a white silk scarf with a ladybird pattern. And a bag of sweets. She said people only have eyes for the baby and nobody remembers the mother. And she said the baby would die and we should stop worrying about him, because if a baby refused to suckle, it was as good as dead already ... Then milk started spurting from my milky breast. I'd always heard a mother's milk had a mind of its own, but I'd never dreamed there'd be so much ... Until the baby finally started to suck on his bottle, and my breast healed and Joe's mother came for the rose of Jericho which had closed up, wrapped it in shiny paper and took it away.

XII

Mrs Enriqueta clasped the baby, whose name was Anthony, to her neck and shouted, chestnut! My little chestnut! And the baby gurgled and she held him close up to the locusts and he suddenly looked very worried. And slavered, brrrrrrr ... brrrrrr ... Joe was complaining about his leg, it was hurting more than ever, because apart from the fact it felt on fire inside and outside the bone, he'd got shooting pains the other side, near his midriff. I've got a trapped nerve, he reckoned. One day Mrs Enriqueta said she'd thought he looked radiant and healthy, and I said he couldn't sleep at nights he was in so much pain.

'You still believe that? He's got rosy cheeks and a twinkle in his eye.'

Joe's mother looked after the baby on Mondays so I could do a big wash. Joe said he wasn't at all happy his mother was looking after the baby because he knew what she was like, and one day she'd be busy untying and tying bows, would put the baby on the table and he'd fall on the floor as he had before he'd made it to twelve months. I'd put the baby round my neck in the afternoon and go to look at the dolls in the emporium window: they had chubby cheeks, glass eyes deep set above big noses, and half-open mouths, always laughing and cheerful, with a line of shiny glue along the top of their foreheads to hold their hair in place. Some, eyes shut and arms by their sides, were inside boxes that were laid flat. Others, eyes open, were inside boxes stood upright, and a cheaper sort always looked at you whether flat or upright. Wearing blue or pink, with little lace ruffs round their necks, ribbons and bows round their bulging waists, and muslin stiffening their hems. Their patent leather shoes shone in the light of day, their white stockings were pulled tight and their knees were painted a darker flesh colour than their legs. They always looked sweet in the window waiting for somebody to come and buy them. The dolls' porcelain faces and paste flesh were always there next to the dusters, carpet-beaters, leather and imitation leather chammy. All for sale at the emporium!

I remember the pigeon and the funnel, because Joe bought the funnel the day before the pigeon turned up. He saw the pigeon in the morning when he was opening the dining-room windows. It had injured its wing, and was half dead and trailing drops of blood over the ground. It was a young bird. I nursed it and Joe said we'd keep it, he'd make a cage for it, so we could see it from our dining-room: a cage like a posh house with a balcony all the way round, a red-tile roof and a door with a knocker. And the pigeon will be our boy's pride and joy. We kept it tied by a leg to the balcony rail for a few days. Ernie came by and said we should let it go, it must be a neighbour's, because, otherwise, it could never have flown to our balcony bleeding like that. We went up to the roof terrace and looked around, as if for the first time, and didn't see any pigeon loft. With that twisted mouth of his, Ernie said it was beyond him. Matthew said we should kill it, it would be better dead than tied up and a prisoner. Then Joe took it out of the balcony and put it in the attic room on the terrace and said he'd make something else, and he wouldn't make a posh house, he'd make a pigeon loft and the father of his apprentice, who bred pigeons, would sell him a pigeon to see whether it would mate with ours.

The apprentice brought a pigeon in a basket. It took three pigeons for it to mate. We called the pigeon we found Coffee, because it had a coffee-coloured marking under one wing; and we called its wife Maringa. Coffee and Maringa, shut up in the attic room on the roof, didn't produce any chicks. They made eggs, but no chicks. Mrs Enriqueta said there was something wrong with the male and we should get rid of him. Who knows where he's come from? she asked. And she said he might be a carrier pigeon that had eaten those funny things they feed them to make them fly high in the sky. When I told Joe what Mrs Enriqueta had said, he said she should mind her own business and stick to roasting chestnuts. Joe's mother said it would cost a lot of money to build a pigeon loft. Somebody said we should pick some nettles, hang small clumps of them from the ceiling to dry, then chop them into small bits and mix them into the soaked bread we gave the pigeons; that would make them strong and they would make eggs with chicks inside. Mrs Enriqueta told us she'd once known an Italian lady by the name of Flora Caravella, who'd lived a full life, and that when she was old and past it she set up a house with a bunch of other Flora Caravellas and put pigeons on the roof, for a bit of fun. And she fed them nettles. And Joe's mother was right when she said feed them nettles, and when I said it wasn't Joe's mother who'd said that, she said, never mind who said it, the right thing was to give them nettles. And the injured pigeon and the funnel were two things that entered the house around the same time, because the day before the pigeon appeared Joe had bought a white funnel with a dark blue rim for pouring wine from the demijohn into the bottle, and he said to take care because, if I had the bad luck to drop it on the floor, it would crack.

XIII

We built the pigeon loft. The day Joe decided to start work, it poured down. And he set up his carpenter's workshop in the dining-room. They sawed the wood and got everything ready there. When they'd finished the door from top to bottom, he carried it out of the dining-room and up to the roof terrace with the balcony and the whole caboodle. Ernie came and helped and the first Sunday when the weather was fine we all went up to the terrace to watch Matthew making an attic window with a deep sill, so the pigeons could think quietly about where to go before they flew down to the ground. He removed everything I kept there: the clean clothes basket, table chairs, laundry chest and peg basket ...

'We're evicting Pidgey.'

They promised that, later on, they'd make a shed to store my things, but for the moment I had to take everything down to the flat, and if I wanted to sit on the roof terrace, I had to carry a chair up. They said they'd have to paint the loft before they let the pigeons in. One of them wanted to paint it blue, another green and someone else chocolate brown. They decided on blue in the end and I did the painting. Because when the loft was ready, Joe always had lots of work on Sundays and he said if we delayed painting the loft too long, the rain would rot the wood. So I painted and painted with Anthony asleep or crying on the floor. Three coats. And the day the paint was dry we all went up to the terrace and let the pigeons out so they could wander round their loft. The white one with red eyes and legs with black claws was the first to come out. The black one, with black legs and grey eyes inside yellow hoops, followed behind. Both strutted up and down for a long time, taking a good look round before flying off. They looked this way and that several times and seemed ready to take off but then had second thoughts. And at last they did fly off with a flurry of wings. One flew and perched close to the water bowl and the other near the food tray. And like a widow in her weeds the female shook her head and neck feathers and ruffled them up and the male opened its tail and circled round and round. And billed and cooed. And Joe was the first to speak, because we were all quiet, and he said the pigeons were happy.

He said that when they had learned how to come in and out of the window, and only out of the window, he'd open the door and they'd be able to get out on both sides, otherwise if he opened the door before they were used to the window they'd only ever go out through the door. And he put in place new nesting boxes because the ones they'd been using so far were the ones the apprentice's father had left. And when everything was ready, Joe asked if there was any blue paint left and I said there was and he told me to paint the balcony railing. Within the week he brought another, very peculiar pair, with a kind of cowl that made them neckless, and he said they were called nuns.

And he called them the Monk and the Nun. They immediately started fighting with the old pair, which didn't want any newcomers, but the nuns pretended not to be there, put up with being hungry and being hit by the occasional wing and living in the far corners of the loft until they gradually won over the old guard and became bosses of the loft. Then they did whatever they liked and if they couldn't, they spread their cowls and chased the others. And after a fortnight Joe appeared with another pair, this time fantails, and great show-offs they were too. They spent the whole day puffing their chests out and fanning their tails, and the next time the old birds laid more eggs, they all turned out fine.

XIV

A smell of meat, fish, flowers and vegetables wafted on the air and, even if I'd been blind, I would have immediately guessed I was getting close to the market. I left my street and crossed the High Street, with the yellow trams going up and down, ringing their bells. With drivers and conductors dressed in striped uniforms with such fine stripes they vanished into the grey. The sun glared from the direction of Passeig de Gràcia and fell *whoosh!* between the lines of houses and on to the cobblestones, on to the crowds of people and the tiled balconies. The street-cleaners swept with huge brooms of heather besoms, as if miles away in some enchanted land: they swept the gutters. And I walked, noting the smells of the market square and the shouts of the market, until I was caught up in the surging tide of women with their baskets. In blue over-sleeves and bibbed apron, my mussel-seller was weighing out one lot of mussels and seashells after another that she'd washed in fresh water, though they still carried and spread the scent of the sea. The dank smell of death floated up from the ranks of offal-sellers. Every bit of animal gut was up for sale, laid out on cabbage leaves: lambs' trotters, glassy-eyed lambs' heads, bodies slit open with half-empty canals clogged with clotted blood, plugs of black blood ... From the hooks hung livers sopping with blood and wet tripe and boiled heads, and the offal-sellers had white faces, waxen, from standing so long next to that tasteless food, from blowing so long on pink sheeps' lights, their backs turned on the throng, as if it were a sin ... Flashing a gold-capped smile, my fishmonger was weighing hake and each shining scale reflected, so small it was almost invisible, the bulb flickering above the basket of fish. Mullet, gurnard, sea-perch and large-headed hogfish, which looked as if they'd just been painted, their bones pricking along their backbone like the thorns of a large flower ... and all that had come out of those waves that had drained me dry when I sat before them, tails flapping and eyes bulging out of their sockets. My greengrocer, old, thin and dressed in black, had two sons who gardened her allotments and she always kept back my bag of greens ...

And life went on like this, give or take a few small headaches, until the Republic came and Joe was swept up in the excitement and paraded through the streets shouting and waving a flag. I never did find out where he got it from. I still remember that blast of fresh air, whenever I remember that day, fresh air I have never breathed again. Never. A blast of fresh air that mingled with the smell of new leaves and buds, and was no more, and nothing since has been like the air on that day that was a turning point in my life, because that April and those imprisoned flowers started to change my headaches.

'They've had to pack their suitcases ... and clear off to the frontier!' said Ernie, and he said the king slept with three different artistes every night and the queen put a mask on when she went out into the street. And Joe said we still didn't know the half of it.

Ernie and Matthew often came and Matthew was falling more and more in love with Griselda and he'd say, when I'm with Griselda my heart goes into a swoon … And Joe and Ernie said they thought he was sick in the head because love was getting to his brain and he kept on about Griselda and it was true he couldn't speak about anything else and was becoming quite stupid even though I liked him a lot. And he said that on the first day after their marriage he was the one who couldn't stand the emotion because, he said, men are more sensitive than women and he almost fainted when they were about to be alone. And Joe rocked back on his chair and snorted and he and Ernie advised Matthew to practise some sport because if his body was exhausted his brain would slow down, and if he spent every day thinking about the same thing, he'd end up in a straitjacket. And they discussed what would be the best sport for him and he said he was a clerk of the works and had enough exercise running this way and that making sure the job was being done properly, and that, besides, if they got him playing football, say, or going for a swim in the harbour, he'd be so tired he'd not be able to satisfy his Griselda and she'd find someone else who looked after her needs better. They argued a lot about this, but bit their lips if Matthew came with Griselda and they couldn't give him advice. They talked instead about the Republic, about the pigeons and their chicks. Because, as soon as Joe saw the conversation was snarling up, he'd take them up to the roof and tell them how his pigeons were managing and would point out the ones that had mated. He said there were some that stole the mates from other birds and others who always had the same partner and if their chicks were healthy it was because he made them drink water with sulphur. And he spent hours talking about whether Pot-Pourri was getting the nest ready for Tiger-Lily and how the first offspring of the first pigeon, Coffee, the one who'd flopped bleeding on to our balcony, with the beady red eyes and black claws, had been born covered in dark speckles with grey claws. Joe said pigeons were like human beings, the difference being that pigeons laid eggs, flew and had feathers, but they were just the same when the time came to make babies and feed them. Matthew said he was no animal lover but he could never eat pigeons bred in his house because he thought that killing a home-bred pigeon was like killing a member of your own family. And Joe poked his tummy and said you wait until you are really hungry ...

And Ernie was to blame if the pigeons left their loft and we let them fly off, because he said pigeons should fly, they'd not been made to live behind bars, but to live in the blue sky. And he opened the door wide and Joe, hands on head, seemed made of stone, that's the last we shall see of them.

The pigeons were very suspicious and afraid that it was a trap and left the loft one by one. Some perched on the rail and took a good look round before flying off. The fact was they weren't used to freedom and took time to take to the air. And only three or four flew up at first. Then nine all told made their escape, leaving the ones that were brooding. And the colour returned to Joe's cheeks when he saw they just flew above our terrace and he said everything would be all right. When the pigeons tired of flying, they came back down and tiptoed into the pigeon loft like old biddies going to mass, heads bobbing backwards and forwards like clockwork toys. And from that day on I could no longer hang my washing out on the terrace because the pigeons dirtied on it. I had to hang it out in the back balcony. Thank you very much.

XV

Joe said the boy needed some fresh air and the open road: he'd had too much terrace, balcony and Grandma's back garden. He made a kind of wooden cradle and hooked it on to the back of his motorbike. He grabbed the months-old boy as if he were a parcel, stuck him in the cradle and grabbed his bottle. When I saw them ride off I always thought it was the last I'd see of them. Mrs Enriqueta said Joe didn't show much emotion but he *was* mad about his boy. And that what he was doing was most unusual. The moment they rode off, I opened the balcony window over the street, so then I'd hear them tooting their way back. Joe would pick the baby up out of his cradle where he was almost always asleep, clamber upstairs and hand him to me, here you are, as healthy as anything after all that fresh air. He'll sleep for a week.

And a year and a half later to the day after giving birth to Anthony, what a surprise! Pregnant again! I had a very uncomfortable pregnancy and was as sick as a dog almost all the time. Joe sometimes ran a finger under my eyes and said, violets . . .

violets ... it's going to be a girl. And I was worried to death when I saw them riding off on the motorbike and Mrs Enriqueta told me to watch out because if I got too anxious, the baby would turn upside down and they'd have to pull it out with forceps. And Joe kept saying, wonder whether she'll break a column again, and if I did the next one he'd put in would have an iron spirit. And he said nobody would ever know how much the dances we danced in Diamond Square had cost him and would cost him. Violets ... and Pidgey's little nose in a lovely bunch of violets. Violets ... violets ...

The baby was a girl and was called Rita. She was almost the end of me, because I gushed blood like a river and they couldn't stop it. Anthony was very jealous of his sister and we had to keep an eye on him. One day I found him standing on a stool next to the cradle, poking a spinning top down Rita's throat, and by the time I got there she was half dead, and her coconut head was like a little Chinese doll's ... I hit Anthony for the first time and he cried for more than three hours and so did she, and both were snotty and miserable. And when I was hitting Anthony, small as he was, a real tiny tot, he kicked my shins hard, in a tantrum, and fell on his behind. Nobody has ever got into such a tantrum as that kid when I hit him. And when Joe and Matthew and Griselda came with their baby, one of them would say Rita was a lovely little thing and our kid would make a beeline for the cradle, climb up as best he could and punch her and pull her hair. That's all the pigeon-girl needed, said Griselda, with her girl on her lap, who was so pretty but didn't know how to laugh. Griselda was difficult to make out: she was pale-faced, with a little clutch of freckles at the top of her cheeks. And cool peppermint eyes. A slim waist. Silky svelte. In the summer she wore a cherry-coloured dress. Like a doll. She never said very much. Matthew stared at her, and melted away whenever he did so ... we've been married so long ... but it doesn't seem like it ... And Joe said, violets. Look at those violets ... Pidgey, my little violet. Because soon after I gave birth, the blue circles under my eyes had reappeared.

To try and stop our son being so jealous of Rita, Joe bought him a nickel-plated revolver, with a trigger that went clickety-click, and a wooden club. To frighten Granny, he told him, when Granny comes, thump her first, then shoot! and Joe was very angry with his mother because she'd taught the kid to say he felt sick and didn't want to ride on his motorbike. And he said his mother was molly-coddling the boy, and it was an old trick of hers and God knows where it would lead. And the kid learned to limp along because he'd heard Joe complaining about his leg. He'd not said a word about it for some time, but after I had Rita he was back on that tack, it was red-hot last night, couldn't you hear me groaning? And the kid imitated him. And the kid always said his leg was hurting on days when he didn't feel hungry. He'd throw his bowl of soup in the air and sit in his high chair, as stiff-backed as a judge, rattling his fork if I took a long time to bring him the liver meatballs that were what he ate most. When he wasn't hungry, he'd throw them as far as he could. And when Mrs Enriqueta or Joe's mother came to visit, he'd stand in front of them with his revolver and mow them down. And one day when Mrs Enriqueta acted as if she was dead, he got so excited he kept shooting her and we had to shut him out on the balcony so we could talk.

XVI

Then that other business started. Joe sometimes felt queasy. And he'd say, I feel queasy, and he stopped talking about his leg, only talked about the queasy feeling he got some time after he'd eaten, and he always ate as if he was starving. And when he sat down at the table, everything seemed all right, but ten minutes after the meal he'd start to feel queasy. Work was slackening off slightly and I thought he might be saying he was sick so as not to say he was worried because work was slackening off ... One morning, when I was unmaking the bed on Joe's side, I found a bit of gristle that looked like a bit of wavy-edged intestine. I wrapped it in a sheet of writing paper and when Joe came home I showed it to him and he said he'd take it to show the chemist but he was done for, if it was a piece of his gut. I couldn't stand it any more and took the kids to the carpenter's shop in the afternoon. Joe flew into a temper and asked why we'd come and I said we just happened to be passing by but he knew why and sent the apprentice off to buy some chocolate for the kids. As soon as the apprentice shut the glass door he said, I don't want *him* to find out because the whole city will hear the news in five minutes. I asked him what they'd said at the chemist's and he said they'd told him he had a tapeworm as big as a house, one of the fattest they'd ever seen. And they'd given him medicine to kill it off. And he said, when the lad comes with the chocolate, you clear off and we'll talk about it tonight ... The apprentice brought the chocolate, Joe gave Anthony some, and Rita a little to lick, and we went home. He came home that night and said, bring me my dinner quick, the chemist said I should eat lots to stop the tapeworm eating me up. And after we'd had dinner he was so sick I could hardly stand it and he said he'd take his medicine on Sunday and that the trick was to shit the worm out whole, because if you didn't get it out of your system from head to tail, it grew back again and twenty centimetres longer. I asked him if they'd said how long this kind of worm usually was and he said they came in all sizes, depending on age and condition, but generally the neck alone was over a metre long.

And Ernie and Matthew came to watch him take his medicine but he told them to clear off because he wanted to be by himself. After a couple of hours he was tottering along the passage, as if he didn't know what to do with himself, swaying from one side to the other, and he said this is worse than being on board a boat. And he grumbled that if he sicked up the medicine, all that bother would have been pointless, and he said that the worm was battling away to make him sick up the medicine. When the kids were sleeping like angels and I was straining to keep my eyes open and staggering around half dead, he shat the worm out. We'd never seen one before: it was the colour of noodle soup made without egg and we put it in a jam jar, in some spirit. Ernie and Joe placed it so the neck was at the top, twisted tight, thin as sewing thread, with its head the very top, small as a pinhead, if not smaller. We kept it on top of a cupboard and talked about nothing else for more than a week. And Joe said he and I were quits because I'd given birth to our kids and he'd given birth to a worm that was fifteen metres long. One afternoon the grocer's wife came to have a look and said that her granddad had had one and, at night, when he was snoring, he choked and coughed because the tapeworm stuck its head out of his mouth. Then we went up to look at the pigeons that she liked so much, and she was so happy when she left. And when I opened the door to the flat I heard Rita sobbing and found her in a state in her cradle waving her arms in a fury, completely covered in worm, and when I'd removed the worm and went after the boy to give him a good hiding, he ran past me laughing in my face and dragging a piece of worm behind him as if it were a paper-chain.

I can't describe how furious Joe got. He wanted to beat Anthony and I told him to let him be, that we were to blame because we'd not put the worm out of harm's way. Because we knew how high up he could reach on the stool from the time he stuck the spinning top down Rita's throat. And Ernie told him not to get into a state, that he'd probably have another worm to put in a jam jar because one would grow back soon enough. But it didn't.

XVII

And work was going badly. Joe said it was playing hard to get but it would come right in the end, people were agitated, and not thinking about restoring furniture or having new items made. The rich were angry with the Republic. And my kids ... I don't know, because a mother always exaggerates, but they were lovely, like a couple of flowers, even if they'd never have won any first prizes. And those little eyes, those little eyes that looked at you and when they did ... I don't know how Joe could scold our son so much. I scolded him now and then, but only when he did something really terrible; otherwise, I turned a blind eye. The house wasn't what it used to be, wasn't what it used to be when we got married. Sometimes, if not always, it looked like a flea-market. Let alone the time when we were making the pigeon loft, that was complete madness, and everything was covered in sawdust, wood shavings and bent nails ... And there was no work around and we were all very hungry and I saw very little of Joe because he and Ernie were up to something. And I was at my wits' end, so one day I decided to find work for the mornings only. I would shut the kids up in the dining-room, tell Anthony what was what, because if I spoke to him like a grown-up, he listened, and a morning goes by in no time.

I depended on Mrs Enriqueta. I turned up, shaking, and by myself, not at her house, but at the house where Mrs Enriqueta said I should go because they needed a woman to do housework in the mornings. I rang the bell. I waited. I rang the bell again. I waited again. And just when I thought I was ringing the bell to an empty house, I heard a voice, as a lorry drove by, and the din meant I didn't catch what the voice said. I waited. Behind the high iron grille I saw a piece of paper stuck with tape on the frosted glass, glass that had a kind of bubble pattern, and it said: *Ring the garden door*. I rang the bell again and heard that voice again coming from a window next to the grille, from a ground-level window under a balcony that was barred from top to bottom. The window down to ground level was also barred and, what's more, there was wire mesh behind the bars that was like chicken wire, although much better quality. The voice said, go round the corner!

I stood still for a moment, wondering what to do, and looked at the writing on the piece of paper behind the grille distorted by the bubbles in the frosted glass and finally cottoned on and looked round the corner, because the house was on a corner, and I saw a little garden door half open, about fifty metres away, and a gentleman standing there in a housecoat, beckoning to me to come to where he stood. And the gentleman in the housecoat was tall with very dark eyes. He seemed a very nice man. He asked me if I was the lady who was looking for housework to do in the mornings. I said I was. I had to walk down four brick steps, which were worn at the edges, to reach the garden, under a thick canopy of that jasmine with tiny starry flowers, the scent from which becomes stifling when the sun sets. To my left I saw a waterfall on the wall at the bottom of the garden and, in the middle, a fountain. The gentleman in the housecoat and I walked through the garden to the house which from behind was a first floor and top floor, whereas from the front it was a basement and first floor. The long, narrow garden had two mandarin trees, an apricot tree and a lemon tree; the top and bottom of the lemon tree's leaves had that kind of disease that makes little balls of white cobwebby stuff where bugs live. There was a cherry tree opposite the lemon tree and, by the water spout, a tall mimosa with few leaves that was diseased like the lemon tree. Obviously, I became aware of these things later on. To enter the ground floor you had to cross a cement yard with a hole in the middle that caught all the rainwater. The cement was full of cracks and the cracks were full of little piles of soil mixed up with sand from which ants marched like tiny soldiers. The ants made the little piles of sand. By the yard wall, next to the neighbours', were four wine barrels planted with camellias, which were also a bit diseased, and, on the other side, some stairs to the first floor. There was a washhouse under the stairs and a well with a pulley. Beyond the yard was a covered veranda, and this veranda's ceiling was the floor to the open gallery on the first floor that was the front of the house's ground floor. Two balconies looked over the ground-floor veranda: one from the dining-room, the other from the kitchen. I'm not sure if I'm making myself clear. I went into the dining-room with the gentleman in the housecoat who was the son-in-law and master of the house. He told me to sit down in a chair against the wall. Above my head was a window that touched the dining-room ceiling, which was half-vaulted, but this window was level with the street and the garden door that I'd come in through. As soon as I sat down, a white-haired lady walked in and sat down opposite me, the mother-in-law of the gentleman in the housecoat. A table with a flower vase stood between us and the flower vase slightly blocked my view of the white-haired lady. The gentleman in the housecoat remained standing, then a thin, sallow little boy emerged from under a wicker chair covered in cretonne cushions and stood next to the lady, his granny, and looked at us in turn. I talked business with the gentleman in the housecoat. He told me they were a family of four: his mother- and father-in-law and a young married couple, the parents of the boy, namely himself and his wife, their daughter, that is; they lived in the house of his parents-in-law, that is my wife's parents, he added. And the gentleman in the housecoat kept fingering his Adam's apple as he talked, and said there were households that only needed a woman to clean once in a while. And such houses were no use to a person who wanted a steady income, because the person working there never knew what reward to expect. So his rate was three quarters of a peseta an hour, but as the house provided regular work throughout the year and they were good payers and I'd never have to ask twice for my pay, and if I liked they could pay me every day when I finished, they'd pay me two and a half rather than three pesetas for the four hours. It was as if I was selling my labour not retail but wholesale, and everyone knows that when you sell wholesale, you always give a discount. And he added that everyone knew he was a good payer, in fact the best payer there was around, not like those wretched people who come the end of the month already owe the next month. I found him quite annoying, but we agreed on the two and a half pesetas and the lady, who'd not spoken a word in all that time, said she'd show me the house, to start me off.

XVIII

The kitchen was next to the dining-room and it looked over the veranda and the stove had an antiquated hood – one they no longer used because they now cooked with gas – which was full of soot and when it started to rain specks of dirt fell on the stove. A glass door at the back of the dining-room led to a passage and this passage contained a very tall, very wide antique wardrobe and, when the house was silent, the resident woodworm began their serenade. That wardrobe was the wood-worm's dining-room. Sometimes I heard them in the early morning, and I'd tell madam: 'The sooner they eat it up, the better!'

Then we went from the passage with the wardrobe into a sitting room with an adjoining bedroom that they'd modernised by removing the glass partitions and simply leaving the archway. The room contained a black mahogany wardrobe with a mirror that was all spotted with age. Under the window, which touched the ceiling like the one in the dining room from where I'd heard the lady's voice shouting to go round the corner, there stood a dressing-table with another spotted mirror, and, next to that, a new washbasin with a nickel tap. The bedroom walls were lined with bookshelves to the ceiling, and at the back stood a bookcase that was wood at the bottom and glass panes at the top, one of which was broken. The lady told me her daughter had broken it, the mother of the sallow kid who had been following us around the whole time, and she'd broken it shooting an air-pistol the Three Kings had brought her kid on Twelfth Night: an air-pistol that fired a rubber sucker. Apparently the daughter, who must be not quite all there, was aiming at the bulb hanging from an electric wire above the table, but her poor aim meant she broke the glass in the bookcase instead of hitting the bulb.

'You see,' said madam.

And in the middle of the bedroom there was a table covered by a sheet that had been scorched by an iron, where the husband of the white-haired lady (the only person in the house who went to work and whom I rarely saw in all the time I cleaned for them) read at night. That table doubled as their ironing board. The walls with the washbasin and window were covered in damp because they were below ground level and when it rained water seeped through and ran down them. The lady opened a little door next to this room; at the end of the passage with the wardrobe with woodworm was the bathroom. They called the bath Nero's Bath. It was square, made from ancient Valencia tiles, and the joins were very badly aligned and most of the tiles were cracked. The lady said that they only took baths at the height of summer and in fact they only took showers because they'd have had to empty the sea to fill that bath. And a dull light came in above the bath through a glass trapdoor that led to the upstairs entrance with the grille and the

notice stuck on with tape and they sometimes opened the trapdoor to air the bathroom and propped it up with a piece of
bamboo cane. I asked what would happen if the boy lifted the
glass trapdoor and looked inside when one of the adults was
having a bath. And the lady said, oh, shush. And the ceiling
and stretch of wall above the Valencia tiles weren't tiled
and were covered in mildew, just like the sitting-room-cum-
bedroom, and it glinted like glass when you looked close up. But
worst of all, she said, was the fact that the bath took ages to
empty, because the level of the drain in the street was slightly
higher than the level at which they'd installed the bath, and at
times when the pressure from the drain didn't draw the water
out, it had to be emptied using saucepans or dishcloths. Then
we visited the ground floor, the flat proper, via a winding staircase; halfway up, a window looked over the street with the
garden door, and when they were all upstairs they'd shout from
that window to people ringing at the garden door to go round
and in via the door with the notice attached by sticky tape. And
from there you could also see the dust-covered top of the
wardrobe with woodworm. And we came out into the lobby,
with the kid in tow, opposite a dark carved-wood chest and a
hatstand in the shape of an upturned umbrella, its spokes full of
clothes and hats. If Joe had seen the chest, it would have been
love at first sight. I told the lady so and she ran her finger over
the scene on the lid and asked me: 'Do you know what this portrays?'

'No, madam.'

A boy and girl were in the centre of the lid, I mean their
heads, big noses and fleshy lips, were, and they were looking at
each other. The lady said: 'It portrays the eternal question, in
other words, "love".' And the boy laughed.

We went into a bedroom with a balcony overlooking the street, immediately above the window from which the lady had shouted to me to go to the garden door. It too was a refurbished sitting room with a bedroom attached. It contained a black piano and two armchairs upholstered in pink velvet and a piece of furniture with very peculiar legs as high as a horse's shanks and the lady said her restorer had made the legs that way to support the small chest of drawers inlaid with mother-of-pearl, and she said they were the legs of a faun. The bed was antique, made of shiny brass with a single column for each bedpost. Above the bed-head was a small recess with a wooden crucifix and a sour-faced Christ in a red and gold tunic, with his hands tied. Madam said that this bedroom was the young couple's room, but she and her husband, the old couple, slept there, because her daughter couldn't get to sleep with all those cars driving up and down and preferred to sleep in the back bedroom, where they enjoyed the peace and quiet of the garden. By the side of the bed with the crucifix was a small doorway to a tiny, windowless bedroom with a bed under blue mosquito netting. There was no space for anything else in what was the bedroom of the kid following us. And we came out into the sitting room where I clapped my eyes on a chest that was blue and gilt from top to bottom, with coloured coats-of-arms round the base. On the carved relief on the lid, St Eulalia, a lily of St Anthony in one hand, stood beside a dragon whose tail curled above a bare mountain, its gaping mouth spouting three tongues of fire, like three flames. A Gothic trousseau chest, said madam. Opposite the chest was a balcony over the dining-room window that reached the ceiling. And on the right, as you came out of the kid's bedroom, was another balcony over the veranda. She couldn't show me the young couple's bedroom that was really theirs, because her daughter

79

was resting. And she and the kid started to tiptoe and so did I. We came out into the veranda on the ground floor that was the flat and went down the stairs over the washhouse and well and into the cement yard that was always full of skittles because the kid liked playing skittles there. Madam told me her daughter needed to rest because she was ill and she said her daughter was ill because she'd moved their pots of camellias. She had passed blood the morning after she moved them. The doctor had said he couldn't say what was wrong without opening her up and looking at one of her kidneys. And it wasn't her doctor, because hers was on holiday, and he'd said that when they were standing on the marble steps in the main entrance, by the trapdoor with the view of the bath with the Valencia tiles. And before I left she showed me how to open the garden door from the street. The door used to have an iron plate at the bottom and bars at the top, but as youngsters threw all kinds of rubbish into their garden, even a dead rabbit once, her son-in-law, that is the gentleman in the housecoat, boarded it over on the inside. The bars and keyhole were still there on the street side but from the garden only the keyhole was visible. This door could be opened from the street, when it wasn't locked, because they only locked it at night, by pulling on the keyhole, putting a hand through the crack that made and unhooking the ring on a chain from a hook on the wall. It was very simple, but you had to know the trick. And if I go on so about the house it's because I still see it as a maze, full of their voices, which shouted for me, though I never could work out where they were.

XIX

Joe said it was my business if I wanted to go out to work, that for his part he would try to make a go of it breeding pigeons. And how we'd get rich selling them. I went to Mrs Enriqueta to tell her about the interview I'd had with my future masters. And the streets on my way, which were the same as usual, seemed narrower. Anthony immediately clambered on to a chair to look at the locusts. Mrs Enriqueta said she would look after the kids, she'd take them to the corner by the Smart cinema and sit them on a chair next to hers. Anthony climbed down on to the floor and, as he could understand every word, he said he wanted to stay at home. I told Mrs Enriqueta he could sit in a chair all morning in the street, because he was obedient when it suited him, but poor little Rita was too much of a baby still. Rita had dozed off with the buzz from our chatter and the boy was back up on the chair and gawping at the locusts. It was drizzling. I don't know why, but whenever I went to see Mrs Enriqueta it seemed odd if it wasn't. The raindrops ran along the clothes lines, and the biggest stretched, turned into teardrops and fell down.

The day I started at the underground house, what a joke! I was halfway through the washing up when the water stopped coming out of the tap. Alerted by his mother-in-law, the gentleman in the housecoat came very huffily into the kitchen, turned on the tap and, when he saw that not a single drop of water splashed out, said he would go up to the roof terrace to see what was wrong; as the tank was half uncovered all the time, they could easily see whether the water was down to the minimum, or leaves had blocked the hole and were stopping the flow of water. The lady said I should dust the dining-room while I waited. Right then I was thinking about my kids locked up in our dining-room because Joe said Mrs Enriqueta couldn't look after them, because she'd daydream, and the kid might slip out, wander into the middle of the street and get knocked over. And while I was cleaning with a duster because the lady said feather dusters only flick the dust into the air and the moment you turn your back the dust simply settles back where you'd flicked it from, her daughter came down and said hello and I thought she looked in the best of health. The lady told me to fetch a bucket of water from the well and clean the window that reached to the ceiling. It was at street level and as cars and lorries were driving past all the time it was always covered in dust, or mud when it rained, a splash here and a splash there, and always kept me on the go. The gentleman in the housecoat came down from the terrace, and from the landing of the winding staircase, which led to the lobby, he shouted that the minimum wasn't coming through, that the tank's outlet wasn't blocked, that the water wasn't getting that far because the outlet from the street must be blocked. Then the lady told me to fetch several buckets of water from the well to finish the washing up, even though she was frightened of the well water because she'd always believed that somebody had been drowned down the well at some point. But there's always the risk the man from the water company will take two or three days to come and we can't let dirty plates pile up that long.

And I was able to finish the washing up several buckets of water later, and the lady dried. Her daughter had vanished. And I went to make the beds. I went up via the stairs over the wash-house. The kid was playing near the fountain, and he thought no one could see him and threw a handful of sand inside and *then* he saw me. He turned white and his eyes were still, as if he'd turned into stone. While I was making the bed in the front bedroom, the one with the balcony over the window where the voice had come from that first day telling me to go to the garden door, the lady shouted up from the bathroom, and the voice reached me via the trapdoor in the lobby, open the gas cupboard, I'd find a card there, folded over, with a crease, and should put it over the notice telling people to ring at the garden door because if the water company man came he might get annoyed if he was obliged to go such a long way round. The folded card would stand up by itself, and they'd made it like that so as not to have to keep sticking and unsticking the sign every time. I slipped the blank card between the glass and the notice and the fold did hold it in place. And the lady came upstairs to see whether I'd understood and she showed me how the glass panes behind the bars could be opened by releasing a few catches, which made it much easier to clean them, though sometimes dirt jammed these catches and you had to shift them with a hammer, and how it was very useful to be able to separate the windows out from the bars because otherwise it was a bind cleaning the glass by putting your hands through the bars. And she said a blacksmith from Sants had made the grille though her usual blacksmith was from Sant Gervasi. But her son-in-law had been able to trick the blacksmith from Sants by telling him he was a clerk of the works on a big site and needed fifty or so grilles for a group of houses he was building and that this one would be a pilot. He could never have said that to the Sant Gervasi blacksmith who knew him well and knew he lived off his private income. And so he got that grille for next to nothing and the Sants blacksmith was still waiting for his big order. I didn't hear the gentleman come in because he must have used the garden entrance. He paid me at one o'clock and I ran home down the streets, and when I crossed the High Street I almost ended up underneath a tramcar, but a guardian angel saved me. The children had behaved themselves. Rita was asleep on the floor. And the moment Anthony saw me he began to whimper.

XX

The water company man came at ten the next morning and I opened the door to him. The gentleman came straight away and said very mournfully we've been without water since yesterday and we weren't able to bath the kid and had a very bad night ...

The water company man, who was big and mustachioed, looked up and laughed as he opened the tap under the manhole cover out in the street. Both men went up to the terrace to measure the water level and when they came down the gentleman tipped the water company man, who shut the cover and went off. I went down the winding stairs and the gentleman, who'd used the garden stairs, asked me to fetch an empty litre bottle and accompany him up to the terrace to check the level of the water because the water man had measured it very quickly and he had this idea that the man was very nice but had left twice the level necessary. We went up, and I held the bottle while the gentleman looked at his watch and a lady on a neighbouring terrace said hello to him and he started talking to the lady who was their tenant, in the house next door, which, though not as well equipped as theirs, also belonged to them. When the bottle was full I called him; he came straight away, with his housecoat billowing behind him, and looked at his watch and said he'd never seen such a lot of water because the bottle used to take six minutes to fill and had just taken three and a half. That night, before I fell asleep, I told Joe the story of the blacksmith and the grille and he said the richer people were the more crooked they got.

After a couple of days I went in without bothering to ring, I just pulled on the garden door and unhooked the chain. I found the lady and her son-in-law sitting on the wicker armchairs by the balcony window. I noticed that the gentleman in the housecoat had a black eye. I took myself off to the kitchen to wash up all yesterday's dishes which were still dirty, and the lady kept me company.

She told me they had a big problem. And she asked me if I'd noticed her son-in-law's eye and I said I'd seen it straight away. She said they had a tenant in a shed and this tenant had mounted a little factory and was making stand-up cardboard ponies in his shed and her son-in-law had discovered that their tenant was making pots of money from his cardboard ponies and had tried to increase his rent. He'd gone at lunchtime and found the tenant sitting down at the table, because apparently they ate and lived in the same shed where they worked, and had their table and bed in one corner. Right away her son-in-law handed his tenant the chit with the increased rent and the tenant said he couldn't increase it and her son-in-law said he could and the tenant said no, he couldn't, until he lost his temper, grabbed the mutton bone off his plate and threw it at her son-in-law who was unlucky because it hit him in the eye. And the lady said, when you came in, we were talking about going to consult a lawyer. And then the bell rang and the lady asked me if I'd mind opening the door because she'd not washed her face yet. I asked her which bell had rung because I couldn't tell where the ring had come from, and the lady said she'd heard the garden bell ringing, which rang in the veranda, whereas the front-door bell rang upstairs in the lobby. She said if it's someone come about the advert in the paper, say we only rent to people with no children, and that the big house has three terraces. If they agree, call me and we'll ask them in and my son-in-law can explain terms and conditions. Open the door slowly, you know it opens into the street and could hurt them.

I went to open the door and saw a very smart, neat couple who were getting on in years. They said they'd left their car by the front door because they'd got tired of ringing the bell that didn't work until by chance they'd spotted the notice and had rung at the garden door.

'We've come about the advert for the big house, you know?'

And the man gave me a small newspaper cutting and told me to read it. I tried to but I didn't understand it at all because there was only one letter and a full stop. Then another letter and a full stop. Two letters and a full stop. And more letters and more full stops, but never a whole word. I didn't understand it one bit and gave him back his scrap of paper and told him the owners didn't want any children. The man said the big house was for his son who had three children and, quite naturally, if he wanted to rent a big house it was because he had children, and then he asked half angrily half jokingly, what should my son do with his children? Call up King Herod?

And they walked off without as much as a goodbye. The lady was waiting for me by the fountain which was presided over by a stone statue of a boy, sitting down, under a faded green and blue hat, and holding a bunch of flowers. Water came out of the middle of a daisy. The gentleman was standing on the veranda staring at us, with a towel round his neck, while he brushed his teeth, because the washer on the bathroom tap had worn out and they'd tied it with a piece of string so it didn't gush endlessly. So he was washing in the kitchen. I told the lady it was a married couple and they'd not liked the fact that children weren't allowed. I told her they'd tired of ringing the front-door bell and that it didn't ring. The lady said that sometimes there were *very* tiresome people who read the note but kept on ringing that bell and then they switched off the electric current and people could ring to their heart's content. While we were waiting for the gentleman to finish brushing his teeth we gazed at the goldfish in the fountain, which went by the name of Balthazar because they'd given it to the boy for a present on Twelfth Night and that was why it was named after one of the Three Kings. I asked them why they didn't want children in the house they were renting and they said children always made a mess everywhere and her son-in-law didn't want that. We went inside and, just as I was walking across the cement yard, the garden bell rang again! That advert! I ran to open the door and it was a young man and the first thing he said was that the house was like a centipede, they gave you an address and then you had to walk round for three hours looking for the right bell.

And my masters always had houses to rent and I was always having to go out and explain the situation and, sometimes, it took three or four months to rent a house because they were so fussy.

I decided to take the kids to Mrs Enriqueta because all this was no kind of carry on. She agreed to take them and tied the girl to a chair with a scarf she wrapped round her waist. And she said she should have had them from day one. I insisted she didn't give them peanuts because they'd stuff themselves, and I told them to promise not to ask for any because it would take away their appetite for lunch. It was a short-lived arrangement. Our kid was listless and kept saying he wanted to be at home. He didn't want to be in the street. I should leave him in the flat. He wanted to be in the flat. And I left them in the flat because it was true that when I did leave them all alone nothing terrible ever happened.

Until that day when I was coming through the front door and heard a flutter of wings and Anthony was in the gallery, his back to the daylight and his arm around Rita's shoulders. And they were very subdued. But the moment I arrived I was rushing around getting everyone's lunch ready, and took no notice. And they'd taken to playing with birdseed. Each of them had a little box of birdseed and they drew things on the ground with the seed: roads, flowers and stars.

By this time we had ten pairs of pigeons and one lunchtime when Joe was on his way back from seeing a gentleman who lived near where I worked, he called in to get me and I introduced him to madam. I left with Joe and, on our way, gave the grocer a list from madam. As I left the shop, he asked me if I'd noticed that grocer's birdseed was the best he'd ever seen, something he'd noticed when we were courting, and he made me go back inside and buy five kilos. The grocer himself weighed them. He was a young man like Pete the cook, tall, with neatly combed hair, and his face had been slightly pockmarked by smallpox. Madam always said his prices were very fair, and that he was an honest grocer who always gave you the correct weight. And he kept himself to himself.

XXI

I was getting more tired by the day. When I came back to the flat, the children were often asleep. I'd spread a blanket on the dining-room floor for them, with two pillows, and I'd find them asleep, often very close to each other, and Anthony with one arm around Rita. But not the day when I found they were no longer sleeping and tiny Rita was going heeee … heeee … heeee and staring at our kid who put a finger over his mouth and said, shut up. And Rita started off on that laugh of hers again, heeee … heeee … heeee … a very peculiar kind of laugh. And I wanted to know what was going on. One day I ran home faster, didn't stop anywhere and got back earlier, and I opened the door like a burglar, holding my breath as I turned the key in the lock. The back balcony was full of pigeons and some had got into the passage and not a sign of any children. As soon as they saw me, three pigeons scurried on to the balcony over the street which was wide open and flew off leaving a few feathers and their shadows behind them. Four more chased on to the back balcony at top speed, hopping and flapping their wings, and when they got there they turned round to look at me and my flailing arms frightened them and they flew off. I started searching for the kids, even under every bed, and finally found them in the dark bedroom where we shut Anthony up when he was a baby so we could sleep. Rita was on the floor with a pigeon on her skirt and Anthony had three pigeons in front of him and was giving them seed and they were taking it from his hand with their beaks. When I said, what on earth are you up to? the pigeons fluttered and flapped and banged against the walls. And Anthony put his hands over his head and burst into tears. And it was a wretched to-do getting those pigeons out of there ... What a joke! It was obvious that the pigeons had been masters of the flat for some time whenever I was away. They'd enter through the back balcony, run along the passage, go out on the balcony over the street, then round and back to their loft. And that's how my kids learned to be quiet, so as not to frighten the pigeons and enjoy their company. Joe thought it was a lovely idea and he said the loft was the heart pumping blood round the body which comes back to the heart and that the pigeons left the loft which was the heart, went round the flat that was the body and then back to the loft that was the heart. And he said we would certainly have more pigeons, because they cost next to nothing and were no trouble. When the pigeons flew from the terrace, they rose up in a wave of lightning flashes and flapping wings and before they went off for a whirl, they pecked the parapet rail and ate the plaster, and left lots of bare brick on the sides of the parapet. Anthony would walk through a crowd of pigeons with Rita behind him and they'd never flinch: some made way for them and others followed on behind. Joe said that now the pigeons were used to the flat, he'd put nesting boxes in the small bedroom. And whenever the kids sat on the floor of the roof terrace, they were immediately surrounded by pigeons that didn't mind being touched. Joe told Matthew he wanted to put nesting boxes in the small bedroom beneath the attic room. It only needed a hole through the ceiling with a trapdoor and the pigeons could have their very own short cut to the flat from the loft. Matthew said perhaps the landlord might not be so keen and Joe said he'd never find out and if we kept the pigeons clean he couldn't complain and he wanted to start breeding so we could start a farm and the kids and I would look after them. I told him he was crazy and he said women were always very bossy and he knew what he was doing and why, and no sooner said than done, as patient as a saint, Matthew opened the space for the trapdoor and Joe wanted to make a ladder but Matthew said he could bring one from work that was on the old side but only needed one or two rungs sawn off, because he reckoned it was a bit too long.

And he put some nesting boxes downstairs but locked the pairs of birds in so they got used to going out up the ladder rather than traipsing round our flat. The pigeons lived in the dark because he shut the trapdoor, which was made of wooden slats and opened upwards when you pulled on a metal ring; from the inside you had to push it up with your head and shoulders when you got to the top of the ladder. We were never able to kill a single pigeon because the kids filled the house with their wailing and sobbing. When I went into the bedroom to clean and switched on the light, it blinded and paralysed the pigeons. Ernie, whose mouth was even more twisted than ever, went berserk.

'These pigeons are in prison!'

And the pigeons shut up in the dark laid eggs and sat on them and hatched chicks, and when the chicks were covered in feathers, Joe raised the trapdoor and, through a small grille he'd had made in the bedroom door, we watched the pigeons fluttering up the ladder one rung at a time. Joe was so happy . . . He said we could have eighty pigeons and when we'd got a good price for the eighty and their chicks he could think of selling his workshop and buying a piece of land and Matthew would build a house with materials he got for nothing. When he came in from work he ate his dinner and didn't even notice what he was eating. He'd ask me to clear the table and under the light with the strawberry-coloured tassels he started to do his sums on an old scrap of paper in order not to waste paper; so many pairs, so many chicks, so much seed, so much esparto grass . . . big money. I reckon the pigeons took three or four days to learn how to climb up to the terrace and those already up there gave them a pecking by way of welcome because they didn't recognise them. The angriest was the white one, that first one that had come, bleeding, on to our balcony. And when the upstairs crowd got used to the downstairs crowd, they'd go down and nose around in there.

The house we'd build for ourselves would be in the high part of Barcelona. Joe said he would keep the pigeons in a special tower, with a ramp that would spiral right to the top and the wall would be taken up with nesting boxes and next to each box there'd be a window and right at the top would be a terrace covered by a tiled roof with a spire and the pigeons would fly from under the roof and go around Tibidabo and the surrounding area. He said the pigeons would make him famous, and when he had his own house and no longer had to work as a carpenter, he'd cross-breed pigeons and one day would be a prize-winning breeder. But, all the same, as he liked his craft he'd get Matthew to put up a shed he could use as a workshop where he'd only make furniture for friends because he liked working, the one thing that got his goat was dealing with crooks, because although there were lots of very nice people around, there were also a lot of crooks and they took all the pleasure out of work. When Ernie and Matthew came to visit, the talk was only about Joe's grand plans, until one day Mrs Enriqueta told me he gave her two out of every three pair of pigeons just for the fun of giving them away ... And meanwhile you are working yourself to the bone ...

XXII

The only sound I ever heard was the cooing. I killed myself cleaning them out. I stank of pigeon. Pigeons on the terrace, pigeons in the flat. I dreamed of pigeons. The pigeon girl. We'll build a fountain, Ernie said, with Pidgey on top holding a pigeon. When I walked along the street on my way to work, the cooing chased after me and buzzed round my brain like a bumblebee. Sometimes madam spoke to me, and I was elsewhere, and didn't reply, and she'd say, can't you hear me?

I couldn't tell *her* I could only hear pigeons, that my hands smelled of sulphur from their troughs, or of seed from when I put it in their trays and made sure it didn't spill out over the edges and came out of the little holes without jamming. I couldn't tell *her* that if a half-incubated egg fell from its nesting box the stench made me retch even though I pinched my nose with two fingers. I couldn't tell *her* that all I could hear was pigeons demanding to be fed with all the fury of their bodies, their yellow quills bristling in dark purple flesh. I couldn't tell *her* that all I could hear was pigeons cooing because they were lodged in my home and if I left the door to the bedroom-pigeon loft open, the pigeons got everywhere and would keep hopping out on the balcony like some game in the madhouse. And that it all began because I'd had to go to work for *her*, because I was so tired and didn't have the energy to say no, when I should. I couldn't tell *her* that I was in no position to grouse, that it was an evil of my own making, that if I ever complained at home, Joe said his leg was hurting. I couldn't tell *her* my children were like flowers that had been neglected and that my house used to be my heaven and was now my hell and that at night, when I took the kids to bed and lifted up their nightshirts and went dring-dring in their belly buttons to make them laugh, all I could hear was pigeons cooing and that my nose was full of the hot stench of new-born chicks. It felt as if the whole of me, hair, skin, clothes, reeked of pigeon. When I was by myself I smelled my arms and smelled my hair when I was combing it, and couldn't understand how that stench from the pigeons and their chicks got so stuck up my nose, almost knocking me out. But I did tell Mrs Enriqueta and she stood there and said I was a coward, that she'd never have put up with it, she'd never have let anything like that happen in the first place. Joe's mother, whom I didn't see very often because she was growing so old and fragile and it was too far for her to come to see us, and I didn't have the time to go and visit her on Sunday, paid us a visit one day because she said she wanted to see the pigeons, that when Joe and the kids went to see her, which wasn't often enough, she complained, they only ever talked to her about the pigeons and how soon they'd make them rich and the little boy said the pigeons liked following him and he and Rita talked about the birds as if they were their little brothers and sisters. She was shocked when she heard the cooing in the small bedroom. She said only her son could have had such a daft idea. And she said she didn't realise we'd let them so much inside our flat. And I got her to go on to the terrace and look down through the trapdoor in the attic room and she went all faint.

'Well, perhaps if Joe is doing good business . . . '

When she saw the sulphur in their troughs she said that you only give sulphur to hens, it damaged pigeons' livers. And while she talked, the pigeons were the masters of the roof terrace. They came and went, flew off and back, walked along the parapet rail, pecked and ate the plaster with their beaks. They were like people. They took off in a flurry of light and shadow, flying above our heads so that their shadows fell on our faces. Joe's mother tried to scare them off by whirling her arms like a windmill but they didn't deign to look at her. The males rutted round the females, beaks up in the air, tails spread, wingtips sweeping the ground. They went in and out of the nesting boxes, ate seed and drank sulphured water and their livers were as right as rain. Once she'd got over her dizzy spell, Joe's mother wanted to see the nesting boxes. The hot broody pigeons looked at us glassy-eyed, their beaks lined up, dark, surrounded by flesh, with two holes for a nose . . . the croppers seemed to be kings, the nuns were all fluff, the fantails got restless and abandoned their boxes.

'Do you want to look at their eggs?' I asked her.

'No,' said Joe's mother, 'they might abort them. Pigeons are jealous birds and don't like strangers.'

XXIII

Exactly a week after that visit, Joe's mother died. A neighbour came to tell us in the early hours. I left the kids with Mrs Enriqueta and told her to do what she wanted with them and I accompanied Joe to see his mother. They'd tied a big black bow to the doorknocker, and it was fluttering in the greyish, early autumn breeze. Three neighbours were in the dead woman's bedroom. They'd removed the bows from the bedposts and the one that was on top of the cross. They'd already dressed her. They'd put her in a black dress with a tulle collar held in place by thin stays and a plush velvet hem. There was a very large, completely flowerless wreath made from green foliage at the foot of the bed.

One of the neighbours, a very tall woman, waved long, thin fingers and said: 'Don't be upset by the wreath that's got no flowers, it's what she always wanted. My son is a gardener and we'd agreed that, if she died before me, she'd have a wreath without any flowers. It was her obsession . . . no flowers . . . no flowers, she kept repeating. Flowers were for little girls is what she used to say. And we said if I died first, she'd get me a wreath of seasonal flowers, none of that nonsense of a wreath made of rare or early blooms. Because I'd think a wreath without flowers was like a banquet without desserts. And so you see, she was the first to go ... '

Joe asked, 'What do I do about a wreath now? She's got one already.'

'If you like, pay half ... Then we'll both have made a contribution.'

And then another neighbour butted in. Her voice was hoarse and she said: 'If my friend was the selfish sort, she'd tell you to ask her son to make you another wreath, because a car can take a number of wreaths and first-class burials always include an extra car for the wreaths that don't fit in the front car ... '

'As my son specialises in wreaths, and my friend knows because he told her ... and he also makes artificial wreaths ... '

And she said he makes wreaths from beads that last a lifetime. He makes flowers from beads: camellias, roses, blue iris, daisies ... flowers and leaves made from beads and sprigs, all in very delicate colours. And the wire he threaded the beads on didn't rust from the rain or the damp air of death blowing through the cemetery. And neighbour number three said extremely sadly: 'Your mother didn't want flowers in her wreath. And she had a very unusual death, a saintly death. She's like a young child.' And she stared at her, hands clasped over her apron.

Joe's mother lay on the red-rose counterpane, like a wax figure. She wasn't wearing shoes and they'd used a large safety pin to hold her feet together, from one stocking to the other. They said they'd removed the gold chain from her neck and her ring and then gave them to Joe. And the neighbour whose son was a gardener said Joe's mother had had some very bad fainting fits over the last three or four days, and she'd said they were like the one she'd had on the day she went to see our pigeons, and she was frightened and didn't want to go out into the street because she was afraid she'd fall down. And while the neighbour was talking, she ran her hand through Joe's mother's hair two or three times and asked, don't you think her hair is beautifully combed? And then she said that at night, when she was still alive, his mother had felt ill and knocked on her door and she and her son had taken her home because when she tried to leave their house, she wasn't in a fit state to walk. And she and her son together had managed to get her into bed … She'd like to have hair like hers.

The lady with the croaky voice walked over to the bed and ran her hand over Joe's mother's forehead and said, as soon as they'd realised her soul was departed elsewhere, they'd washed her hands and face and Father Eladi had had time to give her the sign of the cross. They said dressing her was very easy because she'd prepared everything well in advance and was always showing them the dress in her wardrobe, on a padded hanger so the shoulders didn't lose their shape. And she was always telling them not to put her shoes on if she died and they dressed her, because if what they said was true about the dead coming back into this world she wanted to do so without being heard or bothering anyone. Joe said he couldn't thank them enough and the neighbour with the gardener son said: 'We all loved your mother, she was always full of life and ready to do a favour … Poor dear … Before we dressed her we changed her belt of amulets so she's fit to enter the gates to heaven, if she hasn't already done so, happy, neat and tidy.'

And the neighbour who'd talked the least sat down, straightened her skirt by tugging at the two pleats with her fingertips, and stared at us. After a while, as nobody said anything, she told Joe: 'Your mother really loved you ... and your children. But sometimes she said her real dream was to have a daughter.'

And the neighbour with the gardener son told her that some things were better left unsaid, particularly at certain times ... telling a son just after his mother has died, as you just did, that his mother would have preferred a daughter doesn't show very much tact. Joe said she wasn't telling him anything he didn't already know, because when he was a kid, his mother coped with her dreams by dressing him up like a girl and making him sleep in a girl's nightshirt. And at that very moment, without knocking, the neighbour who'd had lunch with us that day the lunch had no salt came in, holding a posy of pansies, and she said perhaps it was time to get in touch with the undertaker.

XXIV

Both Ernie and Joe kept talking about the patrols and how they should go back to being soldiers, and do their duty. I told them it was all very well joining up but they'd been soldiers once and I told Ernie to leave Joe in peace and not to tempt him into joining up because we had enough headaches as it was. Ernie didn't look me in the eye for a week. And one day he came to see me, so what's so wrong with joining up?

I told him to let other people do it, the ones who weren't married like he was, and I wasn't going to stop him but Joe had too much work on his hands at home and was too old. And he said Joe would soon be in fine fettle because they were going to the mountains on manoeuvres ... And I told him I didn't want Joe joining up.

I was exhausted. I was killing myself with work and everything was piling up. Joe didn't see I needed a bit of help, rather than spending *my* whole life helping others, but nobody took any notice of me and they all wanted more from me as if I too wasn't a person with needs. And Joe bringing more pigeons and then giving them away! And he'd go off with Ernie on Sundays. Even though he'd told us he wanted to get a sidecar for the motorbike so we could all go out for rides, him, with Anthony behind, and me in the sidecar with Rita. But, as I said, he went off with Ernie on Sundays and I reckon joined the militia, because that was all they could think about. He sometimes still complained about his leg but soon shut up when our kid tied a duster round his leg and limped up and down the dining-room, with Rita in tow waving her little arms in the air. Joe got into a temper and said I was bringing up the children like little gypsies.

One afternoon, when the children were having a nap, someone knocked on the front door: two knocks were for us, and one for the first-floor neighbours. I went on to the landing and pulled the cord. It was Matthew who shouted that he was coming up. As soon as I saw him I realised something was wrong. He sat down in the dining-room and we started talking about the pigeons. He said he preferred the ones with a kind of fluffy hood behind their heads and purple and iridescent green necks. He said a pigeon that didn't have that rainbow sheen wasn't a proper pigeon. I asked him if he'd noticed that a lot of the red-legged ones also had black feet. And he said he found the mix of red legs and black feet quite ugly and it was the sheen that was really magic. What was it that made the feathers change colour and go shiny green or purple depending on how the light hit them?

'I've not told Joe, but a few days ago I met a man who breeds pigeons that wear a tie . . . '

I said he was right to keep that quiet because it would be the last straw if Joe started bringing me yet another kind of pigeon. And Matthew said the tie was a line of satin feathers bristling down the middle of their chests making a tie, in a sort of ridge. And they called that kind satin-tie. And he said if Joe weren't so obsessed by recent events, he'd know there are pigeons whose feathers sleek up rather than down and they are called Chinese tie pigeons. And he said he realised it must be very tiresome looking after so many pigeons and keeping pigeons in the flat, that Joe was a good fellow, but when he got a bee in his bonnet ... and when Joe asked him to do something he didn't know how to refuse, because he had that way of looking into his eyes that won him over ... but he now saw he ought to have refused to open up that trapdoor in the ceiling. He asked after the kids and when I said they were asleep, his face looked so sad he scared me ... I told him the kids and the pigeons were like a family ... that pigeons and kids were all one big family. And that it had all started because I'd left them alone ... And I talked and talked and soon realised Matthew wasn't listening, that he was far away, was elsewhere. Until I eventually stopped talking and then he found his voice and said he'd not seen his daughter for a week because Griselda had got work as a typist and had taken her to her parents' and that he couldn't live without the girl at home and knowing Griselda was seeing all kinds ... and the girl's not at home ... and the girl's not at home ... and the girl's not at home ... he kept repeating those words as if he couldn't get to the end of his sentence. Until he apologised for coming and burdening me with his problems, that a man has to face his heartaches by himself, but he'd known me for so long and so well he thought of me as a sister, and when he said that he burst into tears and that frightened me. It was the first time I'd seen a man cry, a man who was tall as St Paul and blue-eyed into the bargain. When he'd calmed down a bit, he tiptoed off so as not to wake the children and when he'd gone

I felt something strange inside me: sorrow mixed up with a refreshing glow I'd never felt before.

And I went up to the terrace, under a glowering, strawberry sky at twilight, and the pigeons ran around my feet, and their feathers were smooth because when it rained the rain ran off their feathers and didn't soak in. Now and then a breeze ruffled their neck feathers ... Two or three flew up and were black against the strawberry sunset.

That night, rather than thinking about the pigeons and how tired I was, thoughts that sometimes stopped me from getting to sleep, I thought about Matthew's eyes that were the colour of the sea. The colour of the sea when the sun was shining and we were riding on the motorbike with Joe, and, quite unawares, I started thinking about things I thought I had understood and hadn't really ... or learning things I'd only just cottoned on to ...

XXV

The next morning I broke a glass I was cleaning and my employers made me pay for it as if it were new though it was already cracked. When I got back to our flat, loaded down with birdseed, I was so exhausted I couldn't take another step and had to stop beside the drawing of the scales on the wall, which was where I always lost my puff when I was tired. I slapped our kid a couple of times for no real reason and he cried, and Rita also started crying when she saw him crying, and that made a trio of weepers, because I burst into tears as well and the pigeons were cooing and when Joe arrived he found us all with tears streaming down our cheeks and he said that was the last straw.

'All morning polishing and in-filling woodworm holes and I come home hoping for a bit of peace and quiet, and find it's all tears and woe. And look at the state of the kitchen.'

And he swooped on the kids and hoisted them up by one arm, and marched them up and down the passage, waving them in the air, one in each hand, and I told him to watch out he didn't break any arms, and he said if they didn't stop crying he'd chuck them into the street. And I gritted my teeth, washed the kids' faces and washed mine too and didn't tell him I'd broken a glass or that they'd docked my pay because he'd have been quite capable of going after my bosses and giving them a rollicking.

And that was the day when I told myself enough was enough. I'd had enough of those pigeons. Dump the lot! Pigeons, birdseed, troughs, trays, boxes and stepladder ...! But I didn't know how ... The thought smouldered in my brain like an ember. And while Joe was having breakfast, with his legs wound round the rungs of his chair, he suddenly unwound one, flexed his foot in the air and said perhaps he'd got a red-hot coal in his knee and it was making his bones boil, and all I could think about was putting an end to our pigeon colony, and every word Joe said went in one ear and out the other as if I'd driven a hole through from one to the other.

I felt the embers burning bright inside my brain. Seed, troughs, trays, pigeon loft and baskets for pigeon shit, dump the lot! Stepladder, esparto grass, croppers, beady bloodshot eyes and red legs, dump the lot! Fantails, cowls, nuns, pigeons big and small, dump the lot! I want my terrace back, the trapdoor nailed down, my chairs back in the attic, the pigeon-run cut off, my washing basket on the terrace and my clothes hanging out to dry on the terrace. Dump the gimlet eyes and sharp beaks, the rainbow mauve and rainbow apple green! Quite unawares Joe's mother had given me the solution ... I started upsetting the pigeons when they were brooding. I used the time the kids were asleep after lunch to go up to the roof and torment the pigeons. The attic was steaming like a hot oven, all the morning sun beat down on the roof and made it fry, add the body heat from broody pigeons and the stench their bodies gave off, and it was like hell.

When a broody pigeon saw me approaching, she raised her head and stretched her neck, spread her wings to protect her eggs. When I stuck my hand under her chest she tried to bite me. Some bristled their feathers and didn't budge, and others scarpered and waited tetchily for me to go before returning to the box. A pigeon's egg is a pretty thing, prettier than a hen's egg, smaller and just right to fit in your hand. I took the eggs from the pigeons that didn't scarper and ran them past their noses and the pigeons, which didn't know what a hand, an egg or anything really was, put their heads forward, opened their beaks and tried to peck me. The eggs were small, smooth and warm after being smothered in feathers and smelled of feathers. After a few days, many of the boxes had been abandoned. And the eggs rotted, still and quiet in the middle of their esparto grass nests. They were rotting with half-made chicks inside, all blood, yolk and budding heart.

Then I went back to the flat and the small bedroom. Once a pigeon flapped and flew out of the hole of the trapdoor. And after a while it poked its head over the side of the hole to spy on me. The croppers scrambled clumsily out of their boxes and flopped on the floor looking anxious. The fantails were the ones who defended themselves best. I gave up for a while but I'd only just started. I'd got to finish the job. And rather than frightening the pigeons so their babies aborted, I started grabbing eggs and shaking them furiously. I hoped there were little chicks inside. And their heads were banging against the shell. Pigeons brood for eighteen days and when it was half that, I'd shake the eggs. The more they'd brooded, the more viciously they reacted. More hot-bodied and quicker to peck. When I stuck my hand under a pigeon's hot feathers, its head and beak searched out my hand among its feathers and when my hand came out with the eggs, it pecked at it.

I was sleeping very badly. My heart kept racing like when I was small and my parents were arguing and my mother was sad and limp, and just idled around. I woke up in the middle of the night, as if my insides were being yanked out on a string, as if I still had my belly button on its cord and all of me was being yanked out via my belly button and one yank and it all came out. Eyes and hands and nails and feet and my heart with a vein down the middle with a glob of congealed blood, and my toes were still alive but felt as if they were dead and that was how I felt. Everything sucked out into an empty space again, through the small tube from the belly button they'd knotted and dried out. And there was a fluffy cloud of pigeon feathers around this yanking that was emptying me out so nobody noticed a thing. It lasted for months. Month after month of sleepless nights and sabotaging pigeon eggs. A lot of the pigeons instinctively brooded for an extra two or three days, longer than was necessary, living in hope.

And several months later Joe started to grumble and say the pigeons were a waste of time, that all they did was grab esparto in their beaks and build nests and stink the house out. And he wasn't far wrong.

And all because I couldn't stand any more, with my kids locked inside, and me washing up in that house where no one lifted a finger, so they could stuff their mouths with clean cutlery, with a kid who'd turned out a little runt in spite of all their fussing ... And pigeons were still cooing on the terrace.

XXVI

And while I was waging my big revolution against the pigeons, what was brewing came, that they said would be a two-day wonder. The gas went. I mean it didn't reach the flat or the underground rooms in the house I cleaned. The first day we had to cook lunch on the balcony in a grey earthenware pot hung on a black iron frame, with holm-oak charcoal I had to fetch, and me on my last legs . . .

'That's the last there is,' said the charcoal woman, because her husband had taken to the streets. Joe was also running around on the streets and every day I'd think that would be the last I'd see of him. He put on a blue boiler suit and, after several days of smoke and churches in flames, he walked in with a revolver in his belt and a double-barrelled shotgun over his shoulder. And it was so hot, so blistering hot, the clothes stuck to your back and the material stuck to your whole body and people were very scared. The grocer's downstairs was soon cleaned out and no one could talk about anything else and one lady said you could see it coming a long time ago and people always took up arms in the summer, which is when the blood comes to the boil the quickest. And, you know, even Africa where it's always hottest must have melted down this time.

One day, when the Sila company milk delivery was due, it didn't arrive. And my employers sat in their dining-room waiting for their Sila milk to be delivered. And at twelve someone rang the front door and they told me to go and open up, with the gentleman in the housecoat behind me. I opened the grille and the man handed me two shiny containers. And the gentleman in the housecoat said, you do see what's happening, don't you? What do you reckon? Can't they see the poor can't survive without the rich?

And the Sila milkman lowered the cover over his cart and asked the gentleman if he wouldn't mind paying – they paid by the week usually – because he wasn't sure he'd be able to bring any milk in the morning. Madam came upstairs, listened to him and asked what they'd done to their cows, and she said she didn't think the cows had joined the revolution, and the milkman said, no, madam, I don't think so ... but everybody has taken to the streets and we'll close down. And how will we make do without milk? asked madam. And the gentleman butted in and said, when the workers want to act like the boss, they don't know how. What about you, sir, do you want the revolution? No, sir, replied the milkman. And he was already pushing his cart up the road and had forgotten they were supposed to pay him and the gentleman called him back and paid him and said he was obviously a good man even though he was a worker, and the milkman said, I'm past it ... And he pushed his cart off up the street knocking on doors to finish delivering his last litres of milk. I shut the grille and the daughter of the house was waiting for us at the foot of the winding stairs, and madam, her mother, said, he said there'll be no more milk from tomorrow. And her daughter replied, how will we ever manage?

We all sat down in the dining-room and the gentleman told me that he listened to the crystal set every night and everything would soon be put to rights because they were on their way up the country. And the next morning, as soon as I pulled the chain on the door and set foot on the first step covered in dry, soft jasmine blossom, I saw madam waiting for me next to the mimosa. Little beads of sweat were streaming down her face and she stood still: 'They almost killed my husband last night.'

'Who did?' I replied, and she said, 'Let's go into the dining-room where it's cooler.'

As soon as we'd sat down on the wicker armchairs, she said, 'At eight o'clock last night, the time my husband always comes back from the office, we heard him shouting in the lobby, come here, come up here! I went up and a militiaman was standing behind him poking a shotgun in his back.'

'Why?' I asked.

'You just wait,' she said with a laugh. 'They'd mistaken him for a priest ... as he's bald on top ... the militiaman thought he'd cut all his hair off as a disguise and he'd walked him like that from Travessera, his gun poking into my husband's back. And my husband said the militiaman was arresting him, and he'd had a hard time persuading him to bring him home to see his family ...'

I flushed red for a moment because I was scared the militiaman might have been my hothead Joe, but then I remembered that madam knew him. But I *was* scared for a second. And madam said she told the militiaman they'd been married for twenty-two years. And he went off saying he was sorry and she said every night they were glued to the crystal set and her son-in-law, the gentleman in the housecoat, wouldn't let anyone else use the earphones, while he listened, looking very anxious, and said he couldn't hear anything tonight.

Two days after the militiaman incident, someone rang at the door at three o'clock. The lady went to open the door and said that the moment she started walking down the marble steps in the lobby, she'd had a real fright, almost had a heart attack, because she could make out a big group of people and the shadowy outline of sticks, which were gun barrels, through the bubbly frosted glass.

She opened the door and five militiamen strode in with a couple she knew, who owned a block of flats on Provença. It seems the gentleman in the housecoat had given them a mortgage years ago and as the couple hadn't kept up the interest payments, he'd claimed the building and it was now his. And the couple wanted their house back and they all went into the room that had the St Eulalia chest, and her son-in-law came up and a slim, well-built militiaman sat him down in front of the table, held the barrel of his pistol to his ear and told him to sign a document to the effect that he was returning the house to the couple, who were the real owners. And that he'd stolen it from them. And if they'd not been able to pay him the interest it was because he was asking for twelve per cent and if he couldn't collect it now, he would just have to sit tight and wait. And the militiaman said, sign the paper saying you are returning the house to this couple, because it is all they have.

And her son-in-law, madam said, went as quiet as a mouse, with that barrel in his ear that meant he couldn't move his head, didn't say a word, and his silence began to irritate the militiaman, and after a while the gentleman started whispering very slowly that the couple wasn't in the right, he'd done things legally, and the couple told the militiaman not to let him speak or he'd persuade him he was right. He could persuade Jesus Christ himself.

And she said the militiaman hit the gentleman with the barrel of his pistol and shouted, 'Sign!' And the gentleman turned to stone again. And they were all so exhausted but nobody said a word and when he'd got them all in a drowsy stupor, he started talking and did in fact persuade them, but they took him to the committee all the same. And he came back at ten at night. He said all the revolutionaries had said he was in the right, but before they'd said that, they'd driven him up and down for ages and were carrying two demijohns full of spirit in the back of the car to set fire to him on some wasteland. And he said he'd performed so well the people on the committee had torn a strip off the couple because they'd wasted their time when they had none to waste. And while she was saying all that a bead of sweat slid down my shoulder like a snake. And next morning, more shenanigans. She was waiting for me at the foot of the steps beneath the jasmine which was wilting from the heat, and she said, 'We thought we were really done for at midnight last night.'

The militia had searched the house because they'd been informed on by tenants who hand-painted scarves with spray-paints in a garage her son-in-law rented out to them because the tenants in the big house he also rented didn't own a car. But the militiamen found only odds and ends in the drawers and wardrobes and left after finishing their search. And madam said: 'Those tenants wanted the militiamen to take us away and force us to live in their garage so they could live in our house. Whatever do you think about the way this world is going?'

It was getting very difficult to find birdseed, and the pigeons started to leave.

XXVII

Mrs Enriqueta said it was out of control and her business had gone to pot. Dump the lot. And what would happen to the money she had in the bank? She started selling buttons and men's garters on the pavement on Pelayo. I saw very little of Joe who hardly ever came home to sleep. One day he said things were looking grim and he'd have to go to the front in Aragón. And he said they'd been able to get Father John out. And that Father John had crossed the frontier wearing Matthew's clothes in a lorry Ernie had managed to find. Here you are, he said, and he gave me two gold coins Father John had given them for me and the children, saying that we'd probably need them more than he would, because God would help him, wherever he ended up, and He wouldn't let him die before his appointed hour. And I put the two coins away and Joe told me not to leave the lady and the gent, they could help me through hard times, and though things were looking grim it would soon be over and the only option was to grin and bear it. Then he said it looks like Griselda's gone off with some bigshot and doesn't want any more to do with Matthew ... A great pity!

He went off to the Aragonese front and I carried on as best as I could, what's new? If I ever stopped to think, I realised I was teetering on the edge of the abyss. Until the day the gentleman in the housecoat gave me that talking-to at one o'clock, when I was getting ready to go home.

'We are very happy with you, come and see us whenever you want. But they've taken almost everything we had and we hardly have any tenants left. We have discovered that your husband is one of these troublemakers and we prefer not to deal with such people, do you see? We listen to the crystal set every night and that's what all you lot should do, then you'd realise you're a load of idiots living in cloud cuckoo land. Rather than waving flags, you'd be better off getting bandages ready for the storm that's going to hit you and break every arm and leg in your bodies. And as he said that he paced up and down the dining-room, fingering his Adam's apple every now and then. And he hadn't finished: 'Don't think I've got anything against you ... but the fact is we can't pay you. I told you right from the start that the poor can't survive without the rich and all these mechanics and plasterers, cooks and porters driving limousines up and down will pay for this with their own blood.'

And he stopped. He went off to straighten the mimosa by the water spout, which was twisting round and getting into a tangle. Before I left, madam said the firm where her husband had worked for thirty years had been taken over by the workers and he'd had shares. And she said, whenever you like, you know ...

Joe and Ernie turned up at lunchtime as if they'd just come from the downstairs flat, and Ernie told me he was in charge of a field gun and had to drag it all over the place. They'd come from the front to see me and bring me some food but they left straight away. Before they did, Joe tiptoed into the kids' room so as not to wake them up and gave them a kiss. Matthew came that same day, and he too was carrying a gun and wearing a boiler suit. He looked very upset. I told him Joe had been there only a few hours ago with Ernie, and he said he'd have liked to see them ... The sun came and went and the living room changed from white to yellow. Matthew put his gun on the table and said very sadly, look at us men of peace now ...

And he was very upset, even more upset than Joe, Ernie and me. And he said he only lived for two things in life, his work and his family, Griselda and his daughter. And that he'd come to say goodbye because he was going to the front and that perhaps God was sending him to the front so he'd soon meet his death because without Griselda and his daughter he'd nothing to live for. He stayed for a while, talking a while, and then went all silent. The kids woke up and came out, and after they'd said hello they started to play marbles in the gallery under a blistering sun that waned, then blistered again. And between dark and sunny spells he said he wondered whether I could give him something to remind him of me, because I was the only person he had left in the world. I hesitated for a moment, because I couldn't think of anything that might serve as a memento. And I saw the posy of withered box tied to the handle of the kitchen sideboard by its red ribbon. I took the posy, untied the ribbon and gave it to him and he immediately took out his wallet and put it inside. And all of a sudden, heaven knows why, I felt the need to ask him something I'd never felt strong enough to mention before and I asked him if he knew who that Mary was ... who Joe had mentioned several times ... And he said he was sure Joe had never known a girl by the name of Mary. Never.

He said he must go and he called the kids and kissed them on the forehead and when we were by the door, just as I was opening it, he shut it by putting his hand on mine and said he had one more thing to say, one last thing before he left, that Joe didn't know how lucky he was to have a wife like me, and he was telling me at a time when perhaps we'd never see each other again, so just you remember me for ever … and how he'd respected and been fond of me ever since that first day he'd come to install our kitchen. And to hide what I was feeling, I asked why he was going away, why he didn't stay, that Griselda was a good girl and would soon see what a mistake she'd made, and he said, there's no way out, there's the business over Griselda, but there's a much bigger business than all that, and it affects us all and if we lose they'll wipe us off the map. He left looking sadder than when he came. It was a long time before I saw Joe again and, thanks to Mrs Enriqueta, I started cleaning at the Town Hall.

XXVIII

We were a gang, the cleaning gang. When I got into bed, I touched the little column I broke when Anthony was born, which Joe had replaced with so much grumbling, and stroked the flowers that stood out on the crocheted eiderdown, and when I stroked the column and the flowers in the dark, I'd think nothing had changed, that I'd get up in the morning and give Joe breakfast, on Sunday we'd visit his mother, Anthony was bawling locked in the bedroom where we kept the pigeons and poor Rita hadn't been born yet ... And if I went further back, I thought about the time I sold cakes in that shop full of glass and mirrors that smelled so sweetly, and I wore a white dress and could stroll along the street ...

And when I'd got to thinking that I'd never see Joe again because he'd gone to fight in the war, he appeared one Sunday, covered in dust and loaded down with food. He put the parcels on the table next to his revolver and rifle. He said they needed mattresses and he'd take two back with him: our kid's, who could sleep with me, he said, and the one from the brass bed I'd had as a girl. He said it was just fine in their trenches and they sometimes talked to the other side, from trench to trench, but if someone daydreamed and stuck his head out they'd get shot dead. He said they had enough food and everyone helped and was rooting for them and a lot of country folk joined them and swelled the ranks, but they let them go when it was time to water the fields or feed their livestock and then they all came back. They spent day after day lounging around, without any crossfire, or talking to the men opposite, sleeping all the time and so much so that he was always awake at night and spent the nights looking up at the clouds and stars and he'd never have dreamed there were so many and so many different sizes when he was shut up in his workshop making one piece of furniture after another. And Anthony wanted to hear more and sat on his lap and made him show him how he fired his revolver and Joe said the war he was in wasn't any old war and would be the war to end all wars. And Anthony and Rita adored their father and he told them that next Sunday he'd bring them toys and country dolls from Aragón, for him and for her. We ate a lovely lunch and then he had to get rope to tie round the mattresses and he went to the grocer, who wasn't very pleased with Joe because he'd made me buy our seed for the pigeons somewhere else. He'd shouted to the grocer from our balcony because he'd shut his shop shutters. He gave Joe a big length of rope straight away, more than he needed, and also gave him some sacks and Joe said the sacks would be ideal for making a parapet. He'd had a great idea for the sacks, they'd fill them with earth, and they'd be ideal.

'You know, I'd be fighting this war with you if I was young like you rather than an old crock,' the grocer told him. 'Now the shop's empty, it would give me something to do ... in my day wars were fought differently. You know what the Great War was like ... nerve gas and the like. Joe said he knew a lot about the Great War, because he used to collect generals on the cards they gave away with chocolate bars. But the grocer said the way young people fight the war now is something I like ... Besides, after that first bloodletting, this is a war that can't ... I tell you, you're doing it right. We'll have peace within a month. I know what I'm talking about. I was always against taking people and executing them and stealing money and burning churches, because they were things that put us in a bad light, but I tell you again I really like the way you are fighting this war, and I'll have more sacks for you when you come back, you know, just give me a shout from your balcony. And Joe said he'd be back next week.

I told Joe what had happened with my old bosses and that I was working at the Town Hall and he said maybe it was a piece of luck because only good could come from working for the people who ran the city. He looked at the empty bedroom that was no longer home to any pigeons and I told him a few of the older birds were still on the terrace. They were half wild from hunger, and I couldn't chase or catch them. He told me not to worry, they weren't important, because life had changed and would change even more, but for the better and we'd all benefit. He left at dawn. The sky was blood red where the sun was rising. The honking of the lorry that came for Joe could have woken the dead. Two militiamen came upstairs to carry the mattresses down and one of them told Joe that Ernie had disappeared. They'd gone to fetch him but he wasn't there and Joe told them not to worry, it was his fault because he'd not told them Ernie would have to go to Cartagena to pick up some banknotes and probably wouldn't be back until the middle of the week.

XXIX

Exactly three days after Joe's departure Ernie turned up, wearing a smart, spanking new boiler suit, belts crisscrossing his chest and back, and carrying a big basket of oranges. For the kids, he said. He told me he'd had to fetch banknotes from Cartagena and the biplane was antique and when there was no weight on board the wind lifted it off the ground, and before the city came into sight, the pilot said they'd never get there flying because the plane was a boneshaker, and the moment he said that, *whoosh!* a bird flew in through a crack in the floor, driven by the wind or sucked in by pressure, and distracted by their attempts to jettison the bird, they landed safely in Cartagena. He then took six tins of powdered milk and a packet of coffee from the knapsack he'd put on the table when he came in and asked me if I'd make him a cup of coffee, because what he most missed as a result of the tortures of war was eating off a decent plate or drinking coffee from a china cup, and he said he'd like to drink the coffee from those hot chocolate cups that had upset Joe so much, and we had a good laugh. He said he was giving me those presents in memory of the fun we'd had scraping paper together. While I heated up the water, he said it was so sad we lovers of peace and happiness had had to get mixed up in this particular slice of history. And between gulps of coffee he told me it was better to read about history in books than write it with bullets. I listened hard because I was seeing a different Ernie, and it made me think about how war changed men. After drinking his coffee, he went on again about the journey in the biplane to Cartagena and said it was something to tell his grandchildren; at one moment they'd had a field of clouds beneath them and the next the bright blue field of the sea and he said when you look down at the sea like that it was all kinds of colours and lots of currents and cross-currents, and when the bird had flown into the plane he'd slid into a corner because the wind was so strong it lifted up the floor and him and everything else too. And the bird lay on his back, half dead, stretching and pulling in his little claws, his beak dribbled its last and his eyes glazed over and shut. And we started talking about Matthew. He said neither he nor Joe dared give Matthew advice because he was older than they were, but when they met Griselda they told him Griselda was a dolly bird and he was too much of a man for such a dolly. And Griselda would only give him one headache after another. But they're things you learn from hard knocks and not from any advice you get. He then asked after the pigeons. I told him that not many were left and they had gone wild. I told him I threw a nesting box into the rubbish every day because the rubbish man wouldn't take them all at once. I showed him the pigeons' room which I'd cleaned out some time ago. It still stank of pigeons. I'd boarded over the trapdoor entrance from the terrace with old slats, and the ladder was flat on the floor. He said, when we've won, I'll paint this room pink for you. I asked him when he'd be back and he said he might come back when Joe did. He shot down the stairs like lightning saying goodbye, goodbye . . . And slammed the door shut. I went back into the dining-room, sat at the table and with a fingernail started to scratch out old crumbs that had fallen down into a big crack in the wood. And did that for a while. Until someone knocked at the door and I opened up to find Mrs Enriqueta back with the kids, who were as pleased as Punch with the oranges.

XXX

Early one morning on my way to work I heard someone call out my name from a passing car. I turned round, the car stopped, and Julie jumped out, dressed in militia uniform, looking pale and skinny, her eyes exhausted and bloodshot. She asked me how I was and I told her I was in fine fettle, what with Joe at the Aragonese front, and she said she had lots to tell me, did I still live in the same flat, she could spend next Sunday afternoon with me if I felt like it. Before she got back in the car she said they'd killed the pastry-cook on the road up to Tibidabo during the first days of the revolution, because he'd got into a wrangle with his family, with a nephew he helped and another he refused to help because he was a layabout, and the latter had got him killed for being a crook and a traitor. And she said she was in love with a boy who was also at the front and she went back to her car and I went to work.

And she came on Sunday and I'd been waiting for her from three o'clock. Mrs Enriqueta had come for the children and taken them to her house because some acquaintances had given her several tins of apricot jam and she'd give them their after-noon snack. I told her I had to stay put because Julie was coming to visit and she was in charge of the camps for refugee children who were coming from all over Spain. And Mrs Enriqueta took the children off and Julie came and blurted out how she was really frightened they'd kill her fiancé and if they did she'd throw herself into the sea because she loved him so much and they'd spent a night together though nothing had happened, and that was why she was so much in love because he was such a good lad and seemed to love her in a way that was quite out of this world. They'd spent the night together in a requisitioned mansion where he did his guard duty because he belonged to some party or other. She said she got there at night-fall and it was October and when she opened the iron gate, she'd had to push it very hard because the last storm had stacked sand up behind it, and she'd walked into a garden full of ivy, box, cypresses and tall trees, and the gusts of wind were blow-ing leaves from one side to another and all of a sudden, *whish!* a leaf hit her in the face, like a man rising from the dead. And the house was surrounded by garden and, heart in mouth, she crossed the shadows between branches that blew this way and that, the house's shutters down, and that wind, and leaves flying and whirling everywhere. He'd told her to wait by the gate, but if he wasn't there, to go straight into the garden because better not to let the neighbours see her. And he was late and she was stuck there as darkness fell and the cypresses shuddered and groaned like the shades of so many dead piled on top of each other, black cypresses, graveyard trees. When he finally came she said it was even scarier because she couldn't see his face and didn't know if it was really him. And they went straight into the house, explored it with a small torch, and it smelled abandoned and their footsteps echoed as if other people were walking through the other rooms and she thought they might be the spirits of the owners, who'd all been killed, and it was terrifying. It was a house of great salons, long curtains, wide balconies and high ceilings and a banqueting room with mirror-lined walls where you could see yourselves front and back, shadows dancing in the mirrors, reflections from the torch all around, and a tree branch crashed against the windows, or brushed against them, depending which way the wind blew. They found a wardrobe full of evening dresses and fur coats and she said she couldn't resist and tried on a backless black tulle dress that billowed like a cloud with yellow roses on the bust and skirt and she said he stared at her and didn't dare say anything and then they went into a long gallery full of sofas and cushions where they lay down, wrapped in each other's arms, and listened to the wind scattering leaves and swaying branches and spent the night like that: half asleep, alone in the world, surrounded by all the dangers of war, and the moon came up and striped everything white through the slats of the shutters. It was their first and last night for everything and they fled before dawn and the whole garden was a tumult of branches and wind; the tendrils of ivy seemed to be alive, chasing them and reaching for their faces, and she took that dress because she thought it wasn't stealing if the owners were dead and put it in a box, and when she was missing him a lot, she put the dress on and heard the wind blowing in that garden again like no other wind anywhere. And she said her fiancé was tall and slim and had dark eyes that glowed like two coals. And his lips were shaped to whisper softly and soothingly. And she only had to hear that voice on his lips to see the world in a different light. If they kill him, she said, if they kill him ... I told her I'd have given anything to enjoy a night of love like the one she'd enjoyed, but I had my work cut out cleaning offices and dusting and looking after my children and all the beautiful things in life like the wind and creeping ivy and cypresses spearing the air and leaves blowing this way and that in a garden weren't meant for me. It was all over for me and I could only look forward to headaches and sadness. She tried to cheer me up, told me not to worry so much, the world would be a better place and everybody would be happy, because we'd come to this earth to be happy and not to suffer endlessly. And if it wasn't for the revolution, a poor, working girl like her could never have enjoyed a night of love like a rich woman. Whatever happens, that night will always be mine, even though I was so scared, what with those leaves, the ivy and the stripes of moonlight and my lad . . .

When I told Mrs Enriqueta, she got very angry and said these revolutionary hussies were shameless, and how could anyone think of spending a night in a house where the owners might have been executed, let alone with a young man, and putting on a lady's dresses to lure the young man on, then stealing them into the bargain. She said one shouldn't do certain things, not even for fun. And she said the kids had eaten lots of jam and while she was telling me they clambered on to a chair in front of the painting of the locusts with human heads climbing out of that smoking pit. It was a struggle to drag them away. And when the three of us were walking along the street, me in the middle and a child on each arm, without really knowing why a ball of hot, raw pain came up from deep inside me and lodged in my throat. And rather than thinking of gardens, ivy and stripes of moonlight, I turned my thoughts to the Town Hall, and good night.

XXXI

Every single light was blue. It was like an enchanted, fairy-tale country. As soon as night fell everything was the colour blue. The street lamps, high and low, had been painted blue, house windows were blacked out, and when a chink of light showed, whistles started blowing. And when the bombers came from over the sea, my father died. Not because of any of the bombs that were dropped; he panicked, had a heart attack and that was that. It wasn't such an effort to come to terms with his death because I'd thought of him as half dead for some time . . . as if he meant nothing to me, nothing I might want to think of as my own: my father had died with my mother. My father's wife came to tell me he'd died and to see if I'd help out with the funeral expenses. I did what I could, which was next to nothing, and when she left, for a second, just for a split second, standing in the middle of my dining-room, I saw myself as a young girl with a white bow in my hair, next to my father, who was holding my hand, and we were walking down streets with gardens and were always walking down a street of mansions with gardens and dogs that barked when we walked by, that hurled themselves against their gates. It was a split second when I thought I loved my father again or had once loved him, long, long ago. I went to the vigil but could only stay for a couple of hours because I had to be up early to go and clean offices. And that was the last I saw of my father's wife. I took away a photo of my father that my mother had always carried in a locket and showed it to the kids. And they hardly recognised who it was.

It had been ages since I'd had any news of Joe or Ernie or Matthew when one Sunday Joe turned up with seven militiamen, loaded down with food, and looking miserable. Dirty, forlorn and all in the same boat. The seven left after saying they'd call for him in the morning at daybreak. Joe said they were eating very little at the front because their organisation was in tatters and he'd caught tuberculosis. I asked if that's what the doctor had said and he said he didn't need a doctor to know his lungs were perforated and he didn't want to kiss the kids for fear of passing on the germs. I asked him if there was a cure and he replied that when you catch one of these nasty things at his age you never get rid of it because the holes spread, and when your lungs are like colanders and the blood you're losing comes out of your mouth because it can't find anywhere else to go, it's time to start getting the box ready. And he said I didn't know how lucky I was to be so healthy . . . I told him the pigeons had flown away and only one was left, speckled and thin as a rake, and he kept coming back . . . And Joe said that if it hadn't been for the war he'd have built a cottage and a pigeon loft filled to the top with nesting boxes and he added that it would all sort itself out and that, on the way back, they'd driven past lots of farmhouses and been given heaps of food. He was home for three days because the militiamen came in the morning and said they'd been told to stay on. And the three days he was at home, Joe kept repeating that there was no place like home and when the war was over he'd stick at home like a worm in a beam and nobody would ever get him out. And while he spoke he poked a fingernail down the crack in the table and flicked out the breadcrumbs lodged there and I felt it odd to see him do something I did now and then, something he'd never seen me do.

The few days he was with us, he dozed off after lunch, and the kids got into his bed and slept with him because they saw so little of him and missed him. I was sorry I had to leave early every morning to go and clean offices. Joe said the blue light nonsense put him in a bad temper and if he ever had his say one day he'd order all the lights to be painted red as if the country had caught chicken pox, because he could play practical jokes as well as the next man. And the blue light nonsense was a complete waste of time. If they wanted to drop bombs, they *would* drop bombs even if all the lights had been painted black. I noticed how his eyes were sunk deep into their sockets as if they'd been pushed right down inside. When he left he gave me a big hug and the children smothered him in kisses and accompanied him to the bottom of the stairs as I did too, and when we came back up, when I stopped between the first-floor landing and mine and ran my finger over the scales on the wall, our daughter said her cheek hurt because her dad's face was bristly.

Mrs Enriqueta came to see me – she never did when she knew Joe was there so as not to be in the way – and she said that it was a matter of a few weeks, that we'd well and truly lost. She said when they'd joined their two bits of territory up we were done for and they'd won and would just keep advancing. And she said she was sorry for our sakes because if Joe had kept his head down we'd have been all right but the way he'd involved himself who knew how it might end up. I told the grocer downstairs what Mrs Enriqueta had said and he told me not to trust anyone. And I told Mrs Enriqueta what the grocer had said and she said the grocer was praying like hell that we would lose, because he wasn't selling much in wartime, even though he sold a bit under the counter, that is, apart from rations. The grocer downstairs only wanted peace because he was scared to death of selling like that and he wanted it over, however it ended. And the grocer downstairs said Mrs Enriqueta was obsessed with the royal family. And Julie came to visit again and said old people were the trouble, their heads were full of crazy ideas and young people only wanted to live a healthy life. And she said some people think wanting a healthy life is a crime and if you want to live healthily they jump on you like poisoned rats, and grab you and take you off to prison.

I talked to her about the kids and told her that we had less food to eat every day and I didn't know how I'd cope, and if they moved Joe from the front, as he'd said was on the cards, I'd see him even less and he wouldn't be able to bring me the few supplies he brought us which were a big help. She said she could help place the boy in a camp, though she didn't advise that for the girl because she was a girl, but it would do the boy good to be with other boys and it would be a good preparation for life. And Anthony, who was listening to us, clung to my skirts and said he didn't want to leave home even if there was nothing to eat . . . But finding food was becoming so tough I had to tell him there was no choice, it would only be for a short period and he'd enjoy playing with boys of his own age. I had two hungry mouths at home and nothing to put in them. I can't describe how miserable we were, we went to bed early so as not to be harping on about the fact we had nothing for dinner. We didn't get up on Sundays so as not to be so hungry. And we took the kid to a camp in a lorry Julie sent our way after I'd done a lot of persuading. But he knew he was being lied to. He knew better than I did that it was a lie and I was the liar. And we talked about sending him to a camp, before we actually did, and he'd look down and clam up, as if we grown-ups didn't exist. Mrs Enriqueta promised she'd visit him. I told him I'd go every Sunday. The lorry left Barcelona with us in the back and a cardboard suitcase held together by a piece of string, and it turned down the white road that led to the lie.

XXXII

We climbed the steep steps of the very narrow, walled-in stone staircase and came out on to a terrace packed with boys. They all had shaved heads covered in scabs and their faces were all eyes. They were shouting and running and, as soon as they saw us, they shut up and stared as if they'd never seen ordinary people. A young teacher walked over and took us into an office and we had to cross the whole terrace through the throng of boys. The teacher asked us what we wanted and Julie showed her a piece of paper and I said, you know, I don't have any food and want to leave him here because at least he'll have food. The teacher looked at him and asked him if he wanted to stay there and the boy stayed silent, then she looked at me and I looked at her and I said we'd made that journey to bring him to the camp and now we'd done that he'd have to stay, and the teacher looked straight at me, warmly enough, and said all those boys had only just arrived but perhaps it wasn't the right place for my son. She looked at him again and I could see she was looking at him and seeing him for what he was: a flower. He'd made me suffer so in those first months after his birth, and it seemed incredible how he was so beautiful, with those waves of thick black hair over his forehead and matinée idol lashes. And the satin-smooth skin they both had. Anthony and Rita. Obviously, they weren't like they were before the war but they were still beautiful enough. I said I *was* leaving him and Julie and I had started walking towards the door when the boy threw himself at me like a cornered snake, sobbing and shouting, don't leave me here, don't leave me here, don't leave me here ... And I had to harden my heart and move him aside and tell him not to be such a cry-baby, because it wouldn't get him anywhere, he had to stay and *would* stay. He'd be all right there and would soon make friends and play with the other boys and he said he'd taken a look at them and they were nasty and were going to beat him up, and he didn't want to stay. Julie was beginning to soften but I was hardening. And beads of sweat glinted on the teacher's forehead and Rita clutched Julie's hand, and said she wanted Anthony. Then I stooped down in front of my son and told him in no uncertain terms that we couldn't go on like that, we had nothing to eat, and if he stayed at home we'd all die. He wouldn't be there very long, the time it took for things to improve and they'd get better very soon ... And he looked down, pursed his lips, held his hands at his side, and when I thought I'd persuaded him and we were about to leave, a repeat performance. He clung on to my skirt, as stubborn as ever, don't leave me, don't leave me, I'll die and they'll beat me up and I said he wouldn't die and they wouldn't beat him up. And we shot out of there, I dragged Rita and Julie behind me, and across that crowd of shaven heads and before going down the stairs I turned round and saw him standing stiffly on the other side of the terrace, holding the teacher's hand, not crying but with a face on him like an old man's.

Julie said she couldn't have done that and the driver, a friend of Julie's, asked how it had gone and I told him and we returned to Barcelona in silence as if we'd all perpetrated an evil deed. Halfway home it started to rain and the wiper went from one side to the other, swish, swish, swish, and the water streamed down the glass like a river of tears.

Mrs Enriqueta went to see my son every Sunday and when she came back, she always said it's fine ... he's fine ... I never had time to go. Rita had a little more to eat but you could see from her eyes that she missed Anthony though she didn't say anything. When I got home I always found her where I'd left her. If it was dark, by the balcony. If the sirens had gone up, by the front doorstep, lips trembling, but never uttering a word. It was like a slap in the face. Like ten slaps in the face. Until the day a militiaman knocked on the door and said Ernie and Joe had died like men. And he gave me all that was left of Joe: his watch.

And I went up on to the roof to breathe. I went over to the parapet on the street side and stood quietly there for a while. The wind blew. The clothes lines which had rusted from not being used squeaked, and the attic door went bang, bang ... I went to shut it. And inside, at the back, was a pigeon, the speckled one, on its back. Its neck feathers were wet from the sweat of death, and its little eyes all rheumy. All feather and bones. I ran my fingers over its legs, and they were folded inwards with its toes curled up like hooks. It had been cold for some time. I left it where it was, in what used to be its home. And I shut the door and went back down to our flat.

XXXIII

I didn't understood what people meant when I heard them say,
so-and-so is made of cork. As far as I was concerned, cork was
for bottles. If I couldn't get one back in a bottle, I'd pare it down
with a knife as if I were sharpening a pencil. And the cork
squeaked. And it wasn't easy to pare down because it wasn't
hard or soft. And I finally realised what they meant when they
said so-and-so is made of cork ... because I was also made of
cork. Not because I came out that way but because I'd had no
choice. And with a heart of snow. I'd had to turn into someone
made of cork simply to survive because if I'd continued to be
flesh, the kind that hurts when pinched, rather than cork with
a heart of snow, I'd never have made it across such a long, high,
narrow bridge. I put the watch in a drawer and thought it would
be Anthony's when he grew up. And I refused to think Joe was
dead. I wanted to think things were as usual and that when the
war was over he'd be back with his gammy leg and his perforated
lungs and Ernie would visit, his eyes bulging out of their sockets,
eyes that seemed bewitched they were so still, not to mention

that twisted mouth of his. If I woke at night, my insides were like a house when the removal men come and turn everything upside down. My insides were like this: wardrobes in the passage and chairs upside down and cups on the floor waiting to be wrapped in paper and put in a box full of straw and the spring mattress and pieces of bed leaning against the wall and everything one big mess. I went into mourning as best I could, for Joe's sake, even though I didn't for my father, with the excuse that everything was too upside down to think about mourning and the like. And I walked streets that were sad and dirty by day, and blue and shadowy by night, dressed in black below a white blotch of a face that seemed to be shrinking all the time.

Griselda came to see me. To offer her condolences, so she said. She was wearing snakeskin shoes, with a matching bag, and a white dress with a red flower pattern. She said she'd had news of Matthew, and they were fine, because though they now led separate lives, they were still friends for the sake of their daughter. She could never have imagined Joe and Ernie, who were such kids, could die. She was prettier than ever: slimmer, her skin whiter, her eyes a more subdued, liquid green, even more like those flowers that close and go to sleep at night. I told her I'd sent my son to a camp for refugee boys and she looked at me with her peppermint eyes and said that she pitied him, she wasn't saying it to upset me, but those camps were very sad places.

And, yes, Griselda was right: the camp *was* a very sad place ... When his time to stay there was over, Julie fetched him. He was a changed boy. They had changed him. He was puffy, with a swollen pot belly, round cheeks, and two sunburnt, bony legs, a scabby, shaved head and a big boil on his neck. He didn't even look at me. He went straight to the corner where his toys were and touched them with his fingertips, just as I'd done with the speckled pigeon's feet, and Rita said she'd not broken any. And while they both played with their toys, Julie and I looked at each other and we heard Rita tell him his father had died in the war, that everybody was dying in the war and war was a thing that killed everybody. She asked him if they could hear the sirens in the camp ... Before leaving, Julie said she'd see if she could get us a couple of tins of powdered milk and some tinned meat. And for supper, between the three of us, we ate a sardine and a mouldy tomato. And if we'd owned a cat, it wouldn't have found a single bone left over.

And we slept together. Me sandwiched between my two kids. That's how we'd die if we died. And didn't say a word if there was an alert at night and the sirens woke us up. We just lay there, listening, and when the all-clear sounded, then we could sleep but we didn't know if we were asleep because we all kept quiet.

The last winter was the saddest. They called up sixteen-year-old boys. And the walls were plastered with posters and I hadn't understood the poster that said we must make tanks, which Mrs Enriqueta and I had found so funny, and now if we came across a scrap of the poster anywhere I didn't think it was at all funny. Up and down the street very old men were marching off to war. Young or old, everyone was off to the war, and the war sucked them in and spat them out dead. Lots of tears and pain inside and out. I would occasionally think about Matthew. I'd see him standing in the passage, as if he was there for real, so real he scared me, with his blue eyes, so in love with Griselda but without his Griselda who loved somebody else. And I heard Matthew's voice when he said we've no way out. And we were all trapped like rats in a trap. We have no choice. We have no

139

choice. Before I sold Father John's two coins, I sold everything else: the embroidered sheets, the best crockery, the cutlery ... the people working with me at the Town Hall bought the lot and then sold it on and made money. It was a real struggle to buy food because I hardly had any money and because there was no food to buy. The milk contained no milk. The meat, when there was any, was horsemeat, or so they said.

And people started to leave. The grocer downstairs said, take a look, all those newspapers and posters ... now up and off ... to see the world. And on that last day it was windy and cold and the wind scattered torn scraps of paper, dotted the streets white. And the cold in my heart was a cold that never ended. I don't know how we survived. I shut myself up in the flat between the time one lot left and the others arrived. Mrs Enriqueta brought me a few tins from a warehouse down the street that the neighbours had raided. Somebody or other told me they were giving out food somewhere and I went looking. I don't know who was. When I got back, the grocer stood on his doorstep and didn't say hello. That afternoon I went to see Mrs Enriqueta and she told me we'd taken a step forward and she was sure we'd have a king once again. And she gave me half an endive. And we were alive and still in one piece. And I hadn't a clue what was happening until Mrs Enriqueta came one day and told me she knew for certain they'd executed Matthew in the middle of a square and when I asked in the middle of which square, because I was at a loss for words, she said in the middle of a square, but she didn't know in the middle of which one, but you can believe me, you really can, they're shooting them all in the middle of a square. And the pain hit me five minutes later and I said very quietly as if my spirit had just died in my heart ... no, no, not that ... Because it couldn't be true that they'd shot Matthew in the middle of a square, wherever it was. It couldn't be true! And Mrs Enriqueta said if she'd known I was going to take it so badly and all the blood was going to drain from my face, she wouldn't have told me.

I had no work and nothing on the horizon, I'd just sold all I had left: the bed I'd had as a young girl, the mattress from the bed with the columns, Joe's watch that I'd wanted to give his son when he grew up. Every scrap of clothing. Wine glasses, hot chocolate cups, sideboard . . . and when nothing else remained apart from those coins that I felt were sacred I swallowed my pride and went back to the house of my old bosses.

XXXIV

Yet again a tram had to stop dead in its tracks as I was crossing the High Street. The driver yelled at me and I saw people laughing. I stopped by the emporium and pretended to look in the window, the truth was I couldn't see a thing: only blotches of colour, the shadows of dolls ... And I could smell that old oilskin smell and it went straight to my brain and made me crazy. The grocer who sold birdseed had reopened. A maid was sweeping the street in front of the boarding house on the corner and they'd put a different colour sailcloth in the bar and there were flowerpots out again. I went to the garden door and instinctively pulled on the keyhole and had to pull very hard. It had always been difficult to open, but it was even harder now after all that time. I finally opened it a crack and put my hand through to pull the chain off the hook ... and all of a sudden I had second thoughts, took my hand out and shut the door, which juddered over the ground, and I rang the bell. The gentleman in the housecoat came out above the veranda, looked down and disappeared, because he was on his way to open the door.

'What do you want?'

He said 'what do you want' in a voice drier than the crack of a whip. I heard someone crunching over the sand and it was madam who'd come to see who'd rung. As soon as she reached us, the gentleman walked off, leaving us alone. And the lady and I followed him up the garden and stopped at the cement yard. The boy was standing inside the empty washhouse and scraping away dried green soapsuds with a scraper. He didn't recognise me. I told madam that I was looking for work and perhaps they ... And the gentleman must have heard me and came out and said they had no work to give anyone, and anyone looking for work should clear off and they'd lost a lot and were trying to get it back and good riddance to those who'd wanted revolution! And they didn't want any trouble, didn't want paupers in their house, and preferred a dirty house to dealing with paupers. Madam told him to calm down, and she looked at me and said the war had been very bad for his nerves and he went up the wall over the slightest thing ... but, it was true all the same that they had had to make savings, or if not look at the boy, poor thing, cleaning out the washhouse because they couldn't afford a cleaner. And when I told them Joe had died in the war, the gentleman said he was very sorry but he'd not forced him to go. And he said I was a red and he said, don't you see, a person like you can get us into trouble, we aren't to blame in any way, and madam came to show me out and when we reached the fountain, she stopped and said he'd become a fascist, she meant her son-in-law, because he'd suffered agonies when they took him for that ride and he'd never got over it and it had made him bitter, and she said he tried the family's patience too. I went into the street and helped her shut the door by pushing it to with my knee and she said the wood had warped again with the rain and that was why the door dragged. I stopped to catch my breath in front of the grocer who sold birdseed; the shop was half empty and there were no sacks in the street. I walked on and paused by the emporium to look at the dolls and a small white teddy bear with a black velvet stripe in its ears and black velvet trousers too. A blue ribbon round its neck. The tip of its nose was black velvet. It was looking at me and was sitting at the feet of a sumptuous doll. It had little orange eyes and dark pupils that glinted like water in a well and with its open arms and the white soles of its feet it looked like a prize at a shooting range. I was so entranced I'd no idea how long I spent there until I suddenly felt exhausted and just when I went to cross the High Street, with one foot on the road and the other on the pavement, at midday, when all the blue lights had gone, I started seeing them. And I collapsed on the road like a sack of potatoes. And when I was walking upstairs and stopped for a breather by the scales on the wall, I couldn't remember what had happened, as if I'd been dead to the world from the moment I put a foot on the road to when I was in front of those scales.

Mrs Enriqueta found me a block of flats where I washed the stairs down every Saturday, and two mornings a week I went to clean a cinema where they showed newsreels about everything that was happening in the world. But altogether it was a tiny crumb of comfort. And one night, sandwiched between Rita and Anthony, with their ribs sticking out and their blue veins showing all over their bodies, I thought it would be better to kill them. I didn't know how. I couldn't do it with a knife. I couldn't blindfold them and throw them over the balcony ... What if I only broke their legs? They were stronger than me, stronger than this skinny old cat. It was beyond me. I went to sleep with a splitting headache and feet like blocks of ice. Then those

144

hands appeared. The bedroom ceiling went as soft as a cloud. Soft cottony hands that had no bones. And as they came down they became transparent, like my hands when I was a kid and I held them up to the sun. And those hands that were clasped coming out of the ceiling separated out as they descended, and my kids were no longer kids. They were eggs. And the hands took the kids that were all shell and yolk inside and gingerly lifted them up and started shaking them: gently at first and then furiously, as if all the rage from the pigeons and the war and the defeat in war had taken hold of those hands that were shaking my children. I wanted to shout but my voice failed me. I wanted to shout to the neighbours to come, to the police to come, to anybody to come and chase away those hands and when my voice was about to shout out loud and clear, I had second thoughts and pushed my voice back inside me because the police would have taken me away because Joe had died in the war. I couldn't go on like this. I looked for the funnel. Where had I put it? We'd not eaten for two days. I'd sold Father John's coins a long time ago. When I sold them, it was like having my teeth wrenched out one by one. That was that. Where was the funnel? Where had I put it? I was sure I'd not sold it with everything else that I'd sold lately. Where was it then? After rummaging everywhere I found it upside down on top of the kitchen cupboard. I stood on a chair and there it was, waiting for me, upside down and covered in dust. I grabbed it and washed it, I don't know why, and put it back in the cupboard. All I had to do now was buy spirit of salts. When the kids were asleep, I'd put the funnel in their mouths and pour in the acid and then do it to myself and that would be the end of us and everybody would be happy because we'd hurt nobody and nobody loved us.

XXXV

I didn't have a cent to go and buy the acid. The grocer down-stairs didn't even look my way and I don't think it was because he was a bad person but he was afraid since we'd had so many militiamen visit us. And I had a brainwave and thought of the grocer who sold birdseed. I'd take him my bottle and ask him for the acid and when it was time to pay I'd open my purse and say I'd left my money at home and I'd come back and pay in the morning. I went out and didn't take my purse or a bottle. My heart wasn't in it. I went out, I didn't know what for. Just for the sake of it. The trams were running without glass in their win-dows, only mosquito netting. People were wearing rags.

Everything was still getting over the long sickness. And I started to walk down the streets, looking at the people who didn't see me, and thinking that they didn't know I wanted to kill my children by burning their insides out with acid. And without knowing what I was doing, I started to follow a very big lady in a mantilla who was carrying two candles wrapped in newspaper. It was cloudy and calm. When a ray of sunshine broke through, the lady's mantilla glinted and so did the back of her coat, which was fly-coloured like Father John's soutane. A gentleman coming in my direction greeted her and they stopped for a moment and I pretended to look in a shop window and I could see the lady's face in the glass and she had big jowls and started to weep and all of a sudden lifted an arm and showed the candles to the gentleman, then they shook hands and went on their way and I walked behind the lady because the sight of her and her mantilla blowing in the wind kept me company. The sun stayed hidden for a long time and everything went very dark and it began to drizzle; even before it started one pavement was wet from the damp and the other was dry. The rain made them both wet. The lady with the candles was carrying an umbrella, which she opened, and it glittered as the rain dripped from the ends of its spokes. A drop of rain fell on the middle of her back and slipped slowly down, and then another, as if it was the same one. I was getting wet. My hair got sopping wet and the lady walked on and on, stubborn and determined, like a big beetle, with me following on behind until she stopped in front of a church, shut her man's umbrella, and hung it on her arm. That very second I saw a young man with only one leg coming towards me and he stopped in front of me and asked me how I was, and I felt I knew him but couldn't think who he was and he asked how my husband was and he said that he now had a shop of his own and he'd fought on the other side in the war and that made life much easier; and I still couldn't think who he was though I knew I did know him and he shook my hand and walked off after saying he was very sorry my husband had died, and when he must have gone some thirty metres, it came to me, as if someone had blown it into my brain: he was the young man who'd been apprenticed to Joe and who'd been so useless.

And the lady with the man's umbrella and the candles was standing in the church doorway looking in her purse for alms to give a poor woman in rags, with a half-naked baby round her neck, and the lady was having difficulty opening her purse what with the candles and the umbrella because one of the spokes had got stuck in her pocket and the gentle breeze blowing her mantilla over one side of her face meant she couldn't see a thing. When she'd given her alms she entered the church through the side door and I simply followed her. The church was crammed full and the priest was running from one side to the other, helped by two altar boys in starched surplices with thick cushion stitch hems. The priest's white silk chasuble was embroidered with garlands surrounded by gilded panels and, in the middle, a cross studded with light-coloured jewels, with red rays sparkling from the point where the arms of the cross joined, which were meant to represent light but were more like blood. I'd not been back in that church since the day I got married. I walked towards the main altar. Patches of colour shone down from the high, narrow windows, some with broken glass that allowed glimpses of cloudy sky, and the main altar was covered in St Anthony's lilies, with gilded stems and leaves, a blaze of gold rising up to the top of every column, to the spires in the roof that gathered up the blaze and sent it skywards. The lady with the man's umbrella lit her candles and her hand shook as she did so and then she made sure they stayed upright. That done, she crossed herself and stood up straight, like me. People were kneeling and I watched them kneel but I didn't remember to kneel myself, nor did the lady, perhaps she couldn't, and the incense came and the incense spread, and I saw the little balls above the altar. A mountain of them slightly to one side of the altar, at the foot of one of the bouquets of St Anthony's lilies, and the mountain grew and grew, some grew out of the sides of others like soap bubbles and the whole mountain of little balls towered higher and higher and higher, and perhaps the priest could see them too because he opened his arms for a moment, put his hands to his head, as if wanting to exclaim O Holiest Mother! and I looked at the people and turned round to look at the people behind me, to the back of the church, all those bowed heads, unable to see the little balls, which were jostling each other, rolling off the altar, and would soon reach the praying altar boys. And the balls were green like grapes and started to turn pink and then red. Got brighter and brighter. Time for me to close my eyes and rest them and wonder in the dark if what I could see was really true, and when I opened them again, the little balls shone brighter than ever. The whole of one side of the mountain was red now. The balls were like fish eggs, like the eggs in those little pouches inside fish, which resemble the sacs where babies live when they are born, and those little balls were being born in the church as if that church was the belly of a huge fish. And if it went on too long, the whole church would soon be full of little balls that would cover the people, the altars and the chairs. And voices sounded in the distance, as if they were coming from the great well of suffering, as if they were splutters from severed necks, from lips that couldn't speak, and the whole church was left for dead: the priest nailed to the altar, in his silk chasuble, cross of blood and sparkling gems, the people covered in coloured blotches from the high, narrow stained-glass windows. Nothing was alive, only the little balls that kept spreading, now made of blood and the smell of blood engulfing the smell of incense. Only the smell of blood that is the smell of death and nobody could see what I saw because their heads were all bowed. And a song of angels soared above the voices from afar which I couldn't understand, but it was the song of angry angels scolding the people and telling them that they were in the presence of the souls of all the soldiers killed in the war and the song told them to look at the evil God was pouring over the altar, that God was showing them the evil they had done so they would pray for it all to end. And I saw the lady with the candles who was also still standing because she couldn't kneel, and her eyes bulged from their sockets and we glanced at each other and for a moment were happy exchanging glances, because she too must have seen the dead soldiers, with the eyes of someone who knew somebody who had been shot and killed in the middle of a field, and I was terrified by that lady's eyes and I stumbled out over the people kneeling down and outside it was still drizzling. And nothing had changed.

And fly high, Pidgey, fly high, Pidgey ... Your face, a blotch of white above the black of mourning, fly high, Pidgey, because the grief of the world is after you, cast off the grief of the world, Pidgey. Run fast. Run faster, so the little beads of blood can't catch you, fly up, up the stairs, to your roof, to your loft ... fly, Pidgey. Fly, fly, with your beady little eyes and your beak below the little nose holes ... and I ran home, and everybody was dead. Those who had died were dead and those who had survived were dead, for they might as well have died now they were the living dead. And I ran up the stairs fast, and my head throbbed and I opened the door, struggling to put the key in the lock, and shut the door behind me and leaned back, breathing as if I were choking, and there was Matthew shaking my hand and saying we have no way out ...

XXXVI

I left home clutching my purse, a small purse, for small change, and my basket with the bottle in it. I went down the stairs as if they led down into hell. They'd not been painted for years. And if you were wearing a dark dress and brushed against the wall, it was soon coated in white dust. The wall was covered as far as you could reach with stick people and names, all half rubbed out. You could only really make out the scales, because the person who'd drawn them had cut deep into the wall. The banister was damp and sticky. It had rained the whole night. The stairs to the first floor had a slight curve like the stairs opposite the wardrobe in my old bosses' house. From the first floor to mine, the staircase was red-tiled with wooden edges. I sat down. It was very early and there wasn't a sound. I looked at the bottle, and it glinted in the light from the stairs, and I thought about the things I'd seen the day before and thought it must have been because I was so weak, and that I'd be better rolling down like a ball, bim, bam . . . and bang at the bottom. I got up and it was a struggle. My joints had rusted. When your joints rust, my mother used to say, your number's up. I struggled to my feet and went down the winding stairs, scared I was going to slip, holding tight to the banister. The stairs stank of feathers. The dustbins in the entrance. A man was poking in all the bins ... Yesterday, when I ran back to my flat, I'd wondered for a moment why I didn't beg. And behave like that woman in the church entrance who'd begged from the lady with the man's umbrella. I could take the children and beg ... one street today, another tomorrow ... one church today, another tomorrow ... for the love of God ... for the love of God ... The man poking in the bins must have found something, because he opened his sack and put his find in his sack. One bin was covered in damp sawdust. There might be something good underneath, like a hunk of bread ... but what good is a hunk of bread when you are starving? If you want to eat grass you need the strength to go and look for grass and then what is grass at the end of the day ... ? I had learned to read and write and my mother brought me up to wear clean clothes. I had learned to read and write and I had sold cakes and sweets and bars of dark chocolate and liqueur chocolates. And I walked along the street as ordinary as anybody else. I had learned to read and write and had served and helped ... A drop of water splashed on my nose from a balcony. I crossed the High Street. There were now goods on sale in some shops and people in the street who could go into that handful of shops to buy. And I thought of these things to keep my mind off the shiny green bottle in my basket. And I looked at everything as if I was seeing it for the first time, because tomorrow I wouldn't be able to, it's not I who looks, who speaks, who sees. Tomorrow nothing pretty or ugly would meet these eyes. Things did now, everything passed before my eyes as if to register there for ever, before I died. And my glassy eyes took

everything in. The teddy bear had disappeared from the emporium window and when I saw it had gone I longed to see it there
in its velvet breeches, sitting there like a prize target. The smell
of feathers from the bins stayed in my nose until I walked past
the perfume shop and the smell of soap and sweet eau de
cologne wafted out. I was gradually getting nearer to the grocer
who sold birdseed. There were no sacks in the street. At that
time of day, in my old bosses' house, madam would be getting
breakfast ready and the boy would be playing skittles in the
yard. The drizzle would be soaking the basement walls and more
mould would grow on the damp patches and sparkle like salt.
The grocer was behind the counter serving two young maids
and a lady. I thought I recognised one of the maids by sight. The
grocer saw to the lady and the two girls and my legs were hurting from standing up so long. When it was my turn, another
maid came in. I put the bottle on the counter and said: spirit of
salts. And when it was time to pay, the bottle was still steaming
between the bottle and the cork, I opened my purse, let them
see my surprise and said I'd left my small change at home. The
grocer said not to worry, no need to come specially to pay, I
could pay when I next came that way, any time, when it suited
me. He asked after my bosses and I told him I'd not worked
there for some time, since the start of the war, and he said he'd
also fought in the war and it was a miracle he'd been able to
open his shop again, and he came out from behind the counter
and put the bottle of acid in my basket. I breathed as if the
world was now mine. And I left. I had to make sure I didn't
stumble, didn't get knocked over, had to take care with the
trams, particularly the ones coming downhill, not lose my nerve
and go straight home and not see any blue lights. I looked in the
perfumery window once again, at the bottles of yellow eau de

cologne and the nail scissors that were so new and shiny and the small boxes with little mirrors in the lid, and a little bar of black soap and a little brush to do your eyelashes.

And back to the emporium and the dolls with the patent leather shoes ... above all I mustn't see blue lights and not cross in a hurry ... must not see the blue lights ... and someone shouted to me. Someone shouted to me and I turned round, and it was the birdseed grocer shouting and walking towards me and when I turned round I thought of the salt woman. I thought the grocer had realised he'd given me bleach and not spirit of salts and I didn't know what to think. He asked me if I'd come back to the shop with him, he was sorry, and we went into the shop which was now empty and he asked me if I'd like to do house-work for him, that he'd known me for some time, that the woman who'd cleaned for him had stopped because she was too old and worn out ... And then someone came in and he said, wait for a moment, and then he was back waiting for my reply. And when I didn't say anything he asked if perhaps I already had work and wasn't free, and I shook my head and said I didn't know what to say. He said if I didn't have any work, his was a good house and not too much bother and he already knew I was a reliable worker. I nodded and then he said, you can start tomorrow, and with a look of concern he fetched two tins from inside and put them in my basket, and a packet of milk, and something else I've forgotten. And he said I could start in the morning at nine. And I instinctively took the bottle out of my basket and put it gingerly on the counter. And I left without saying a word. And when I was back in the flat, I burst into tears like any old poor soul, me, someone who always found it hard to cry.

XXXVII

There were acorns and leaves and an ink stain in the middle hidden under a brass vase with a scene of lightly clad ladies making a garland, their hair loose and blowing in the wind, and a vase of dried red roses and daisies set in a lump of moulded moss. The fringe on the tablecloth with the acorns and ink stain had three rows of knots. The sideboard was reddish wood with a pink marble top under the glassware cupboard. I mean the wine glasses and water jug and wine bottle that were just for show. A window that was always dark looked down on an inside yard, as did the kitchen window. It was a dining-room, *the* dining-room, and had two windows, because another window looked down into the shop and was always open so the grocer could keep an eye on what was happening in the shop when he was in the dining-room. The chairs were Viennese style and their seats and backs were full of little holes. Aren't you tired, the grocer was always asking, who was an Anthony like my son. I told him I was no stranger to hard work, and one day I told him I'd worked in a pastry shop as a young girl. He liked to talk to me from time to time. You could hardly see his smallpox scars in the dim dining-room light. The doorway into the shop didn't have a door. It was an empty space to go in and out of, in which the grocer had hung a bamboo curtain with a painting of a Japanese woman with a mountain of hair like a pincushion holding a fan handpainted with distant birds and, in the foreground, a lit lantern.

Apart from the two bedrooms looking over the street to the market, it was a simple house full of shadows. It was like this: a passage ran from the curtain with the Japanese lady to the other end of the house where there was a sitting room with a settee and armchairs with covers and a console table. On the left of the passage, two doors, next to each other, led into two bedrooms with windows over the street to the market. On the right, the kitchen and a windowless room, the stockroom, full of sacks of grain and potatoes, and bottles. And that was it for the passage. At the end of the passage was the sitting room; and to its right, the grocer's bedroom which was as big as the sitting room, with a veranda with windows beneath the first-floor balcony which was supported by four wrought-iron columns. Beyond the veranda was a dusty yard, divided from the first floor's garden by a spiked fence. This yard was always full of litter and rubbish from the other flats. The first-floor garden had a single tree: a stunted peach. The peaches were no bigger than hazels when they fell to the ground. And next to the first-floor's garden fence, a small barred gate that would only half shut and led to the street down to the market. To get back to the sitting room, the console held a mirror with a wooden frieze at the top. And two bell jars that contained wild flowers: poppies, ears of wheat, cornflowers and wild roses. And between the bell jars, a conch-shell, the kind that sounds like the sea if you put it next to your ear. That shell must have contained every roar of the sea and I felt it was stronger than any person, because no one could ever have withstood those waves swirling backwards and forwards inside. And when I dusted it, I always listened in for a while.

The red floor tiles in the house were the sort that get covered in dust the moment you've scrubbed them. One of the first things the grocer told me was to be very careful not to leave the doors to the sitting room and bedroom verandas open, because that's how the rats got in. Little rats with long skinny legs. Hunchbacked rats. They came out of the drain near the bottom of the barred gate in the yard, ran into the store and gnawed the sacks and ate the grain on the sly. And it wouldn't have been so bad if they'd only eaten the grain, even though that was in short supply; the worst was when he or an assistant fetched a sack for the shop and as they dragged it along the floor the grain scattered all over the place, and it was a real bother shovelling it back up. His assistant ate and lived on the first floor. He lived in because the grocer didn't want strangers in his house once he'd pulled his metal shutters down.

The grocer slept in a double bed and later he told me it had been his parents' bed and he always felt the bed smelled of his family and of his mother's hands when she baked apples on the fire for him at the start of winter. It was a black bed with columns that were thin, bulged, then grew thin again and turned into a ball, and the top of the column above the ball went thin, bulged, then grew thin again. The eiderdown was almost a twin to the one I used to have and had been forced to sell: crocheted with roses that stuck out and with a tasselled fringe you could wash and iron, which either unravelled or curled up again as if it had a mind of its own. And there was a screen in one corner for undressing behind.

XXXVIII

It was a struggle to lift my spirits, but they gradually revived after a time of flirting with death. The kids no longer looked as if they were skin and bone. And the blue of their veins didn't stand out so. I was paying off the rent I owed, not with the money I was earning but with the money I was saving, because at the end of the day the grocer always said, here, take this: a split bag of rice, a bag of chickpeas. And he always said he'd got more than his fair share of rations. The shop wasn't back to its pre-war standard, but it was a good shop ... And some scraps from the first cut of a ham or a salami, so the vegetables didn't feel lonely ... Lots of things. Lots. It is difficult to describe what that meant for us. I'd leave with my paper bags and run up to our flat, always touching the scales on my way. And the kids were waiting for me and welcomed me with wide eyes, what've you brought today? And I'd put the bags on the table and between us we'd take out the vegetables and if there were any stones among the lentils, they'd bounce them on the floor and then collect them up. And when it was warm at night, we'd go up to the roof terrace and sit on the floor with me in the middle, like when we were asleep in bed. And when it was really hot, we sometimes dozed off there until daylight glowed red in our eyes and woke us and we'd run down to the flat, eyes half closed so as not to wake up, and sleep on a blanket because we didn't own a mattress. And we slept until it was time to get up. The kids never mentioned their father, as if he'd never existed. And I did remember him from time to time, but I'd make a big effort to put him out of my mind because I found it exhausting, I can't describe how much, and I had to get on with life, and if I thought too hard, my brain hurt as if it had gone rotten.

When I'd been working for a good few months at the grocer's, perhaps thirteen or fifteen … a good few months cleaning his house so it shone like a pin, all the furniture polished with a mixture of oil and vinegar and the eiderdown whiter than the whitest teeth and the armchair and settee covers laundered and ironed, the birdseed grocer asked me if my kids went to school, and I said that for the moment they didn't. And one day he said he'd noticed me the first time I went in the shop to buy birdseed, and Joe as well, he said, a lad who always stayed in the street with his hands in his pockets, looking this way and that. And I asked him how he could see if he was behind the counter, and he said, don't you remember I had those sacks in the street? And even if I hadn't had them and didn't go out to get seed, I'd have seen him anyway, because he said he kept a mirror behind the counter that was placed in such a way as to enable him to keep an eye out to make sure nobody was thieving. And that mirror meant he could move around the shop and still see the sacks in the street and whether children put their hands in and took out loads. And he said I shouldn't be upset, but the day he ran after me to ask me if I wanted to clean for him, he'd done so because the look on my face had frightened him and he thought I must be having a really bad time. And I told him I wasn't really. Only that Joe had been killed in the war and life wasn't easy and he said he'd fought in the war as well and been in hospital for a year. That he'd been rescued half dead from the battlefield and they'd patched him up as best they could and then he said, come at three on Sunday. And added that he thought that, as he was getting on, I wouldn't be worried about being alone with him, and, after all, I had known him for quite some time.

XXXIX

I ran my fingers over the scales as I went downstairs and out into the street. It was a cloudy Sunday afternoon, no air or sun, no rain either. I found it difficult to breathe, like a fish just hooked out of the sea. The grocer had told me to go in through the yard gate, which would be open as usual because it was the only entrance you could use on a Sunday. He wasn't going to spend his time raising and lowering the shutters when he had visitors. And I don't know why, but I was going to see him, and I *had* made my mind up to go, proof was the fact that I was now on my way. I walked in fits and starts and wasted time staring at myself in all the shop windows and watching myself walk in them, where everything was darker and shinier. My hair was irritating me. I'd cut and washed it myself and I felt it was a bit out of control.

He was waiting for me, standing between two of the four columns that supported the back balconies of the six flats. As I went in, an aeroplane made out of newspaper whirled down from the balcony of one of the top-floor flats. The grocer caught it mid-flight and said it was better not to say anything because if he complained, they might get angry and throw even more things at him. You could see he'd just shaved and nicked himself below one ear. In that cloudy light the pockmarks seemed to have sunk deeper into his cheeks. Each little round hole had a fresher, lighter tone than the skin you're born with.

He asked if I wouldn't mind going in. And he made me go in first, and it seemed odd because everything was different without the bright light that came through the bamboo curtain from the open shop on other days of the week and it was as if it was another house. The light was on in the dining-room, the light being an upside-down porcelain bowl hanging from the ceiling on six brass chains. Small glass tubes, white like the bowl, hung from its rim. Sometimes, if people ran across the flat upstairs, they tinkled a little tune. And we went into the dining-room and sat down.

'Would you like a biscuit?'

He placed a square box of biscuits in front of me, layer upon layer of vanilla biscuits, and I pushed them away, saying thank you very much but I'm not very hungry. He asked after the children and, while he was talking and putting the biscuits back in the sideboard, where they belonged, I realised he was finding it an effort to do and say what he wanted to do and say, and I felt he was like a sea creature with a cracked shell, and that is as forlorn as you can get. He apologised for asking me to come on a Sunday, no doubt the day I should be at home tidying and spending time with my children. And right then we heard them running upstairs and the glass tubes tinkling ... We looked at the light swinging through the air and when the tubes stopped jingling I told him to tell me whatever was on his mind, that is, if he had something to tell me. And he said it was all very difficult. And he put his hands on the table and locked the fingers of both hands together and when he'd done that good and tight, and his knuckles had gone white, he said he was quite at a loss. Because he led a simple life, shut up there, endlessly tidying the shop, working away, cleaning, watching the sacks in the store to make sure the rats didn't nibble them, because a rat once made a nest in a bundle of dishcloths and the rat dirtied on the cloths and he'd not noticed, even though he'd killed the rat and its babies, and the girl put the cloths on sale. And a maid, who smiled sweetly, though he didn't like her one bit, bought two dishcloths and soon after the maid came back with her mistress in tow and they complained loudly because they couldn't believe he was so careless as to sell dishcloths, cloths for washing the dishes, that were covered in rat dirt. And that story about the dishcloths was just to show me I should be careful the rats that came out of the drain didn't get in through the yard. He said his life wasn't much fun, that it wasn't a life to offer up as something wonderful, it simply boiled down to work and saving for your old age. He said he thought a lot about old age and wanted to be an old man people respected and the old were only respected if they had a livelihood. He said he wasn't a man who liked to go without, but he thought a lot about old age and when he hadn't hair or teeth, or energy in his legs or strength to put his shoes on, he didn't want to be forced to knock on the workhouse door and end up living there after a life spent toiling and struggling day in day out. He unlocked his fingers and put two into the vase hiding the ink stain, and took out a pinch of moss from between the red roses and daisies and looked away from me and said he thought a lot about me and my children and believed a lot in people being fated ... and he'd asked me to come on a Sunday in order to talk with a little more peace and quiet, because he wanted to ask me something, and he didn't know how to start, particularly because he didn't know how I would react. And they started running across the flat upstairs again, and more tinkling, and he said, as long as they don't make our ceiling cave in … And he said that as if I also belonged there … And he said he was a man who lived on his own. All on his own, with no parents or family of any kind. As lonely as the falling rain. And I could trust him and shouldn't be at all upset by what he wanted to say … And he wanted to say he wasn't the kind of man who could live by himself … And he fell silent for a good long time and then looked up, stared at me and said, I want to marry you, but I can't start a family …

And he banged a fist loudly on the table. That was what he said, he couldn't start a family and he wanted to get married. And he rolled the moss he'd taken from the brass vase into a little green ball. He got up and looked at the Japanese woman, then turned round and sat down again, and, as he was sitting down, but hadn't quite, he asked, 'Would you like to marry me?'

I'd been afraid that was what he'd been leading up to, but even though I'd been afraid that was what was coming, I was still very shocked and didn't really understand.

'I am free, you are free, I need company and your children need a helping hand … '

He got up, seeming much tenser than I was, and walked through the Japanese woman two or three times, in and out of the dining-room … And as he sat down again he told me I couldn't possibly know how kind he was. That I didn't know what a good man he was. And he'd always felt affection towards me, from the time I came to buy birdseed and he saw me carrying a load I could hardly manage.

'I think of you all alone and your children locked inside and

all alone while you are at work, and I could change all that ...
If you don't like the idea, then behave as if I'd never said a
word ... But I should repeat that I can't start a family, because
the war made me useless from the waist down, and you'd bring
me a ready-made family. And I don't want to mislead anyone,'
he said. 'Natalia.'

XL

I went up to our flat feeling quite light-headed and, although I didn't want to go and didn't want to blab to anyone, by ten o'clock it was too much for me. I grabbed the kids and rushed off to Mrs Enriqueta, who was already doing her hair and getting ready for bed. I sat my kids in front of the locusts and told them to take a good look while I closeted myself in the kitchen with Mrs Enriqueta. I told her what was wrong and told her I thought I'd understood though I didn't think I'd really got to the bottom of what he was saying. And she said, he must have been maimed in the war, and it's exactly what you think it is and that's why he wants to marry you because you bring him a ready-made family, and lots of men who don't have a family feel like an empty bottle adrift at sea.

'And what should I tell the kids?'

'You tell them right away you've said yes as if it was the most natural thing in the world. And what do they know ... ?'

I thought about it for several days and the day I decided, after weighing up all the pros and cons, I said yes to the grocer, let's get married. I said I'd taken my time because he'd taken me by surprise and as time passed I'd felt even more surprised, and out of respect for my kids who were older than their years, because hunger and the war had helped them to understand the world better. He took my hand in his trembling one and said I couldn't imagine how happy I'd made him. And I went off to do the housework. I stood on sunlit tiles by a balcony. A shadow flew from the peach tree. It was a bird. And a cloud of dust fell down into the yard from the balconies. I found a cobweb in the room with the bell jars. It looped from one jar to the other. It started from the wooden pedestal, passed over the conch-shell and ended on the base of the other bell jar. And I surveyed what would soon be my home. And felt a lump in my throat. Because I'd wanted to say no, as soon as I'd said yes. I didn't like the place one bit, the shop, the passage that was like a dingy intestine, or the rats that came out of the drain. I told the children at midday. Not exactly that I was getting married but that we were going to live in another house and a gentleman who was a very good man would see to it that they went to school. Neither said a word, though I think they understood. They'd got used to not saying a word and their eyes had become very sad.

And three months after that Sunday, early one morning I married Anthony who from that day on became Anthony-dad and my son Anthony-son, though we soon got round to calling him Tony.

But he refurbished the house before we married. I said I wanted brass bedsteads for the kids and I got brass bedsteads, like the one I had had since I was a young girl and had been forced to sell. I said I wanted a kitchen range and I got a kitchen range. I said I wanted a tablecloth without an ink stain and I got one. And one day I told him I might still be poor but I had my feelings and I'd prefer not to take a single miserable item from my old house to my new house: not even clothes. And we got everything new and when I said I might still be poor but I had my feelings, he replied he was no different. And that was true.

XLI

And the children started studying, each in their own bedroom, with a window, a brass bedstead, a white counterpane, with a yellow eiderdown in winter, and a white table and their own little armchair. The day after we married, Anthony said he didn't want to see me spend another five minutes cleaning. I should look for a cleaning lady to come in the morning and if I wanted, a housemaid in the afternoon. He'd not married me so I could wash his clothes but to have a family, as he'd said, and he wanted to see his family happy. We had everything. Clothes, crockery, cutlery and scented soap. And as the bedrooms were freezing in winter and cold in other months, we all wore bed-socks, except in the middle of summer.

Mrs Enriqueta came to see me and, like the first time, begged me all over again to tell her what the wedding night had been like and how we'd managed not being able to do it. And she laughed. When she first visited, we sat next to each other on the covered settee but later we both sat on armchairs because she said the settee sagged too much and a stay from her corset stuck into her armpit. She sat very strangely: feet together and knees apart, sitting very upright, her angler-fish mouth and paper cone of a nose looking down. I showed her everything I had, clothes to wear outside and in, and she said the shop couldn't possibly reach to all that, Anthony must have money tucked away, and I told her I didn't know. And she was very shocked by the screen. What an idea, she said. And when I told her I had a cleaning lady she said it was only what I deserved. I said her name was Rosa and, sometimes, Mrs Enriqueta would come early to see Rosa, especially the day when Rosa ironed, always in the room with the covered settee, because she so liked to watch her iron. When Mrs Enriqueta left she went out through the shop and, from the start, he gave her a small packet of biscuits each time, and won her over, so much so that when she came she could only talk about Anthony and look at him lovingly as if he was hers.

One day we caught a tiny rat. I found it in a trap early one afternoon. I was the one who noticed it. I summoned everyone out into the yard. It had been caught in one of those traps that snaps to and had been sliced down the middle. It had burst open and bits of bloody intestine were hanging out and in the hole at its rear end you could see the snout of a baby rat about to be born. It was very fragile – its colour, little toes and the white skin on its tummy that wasn't really white though it looked as if it was because it was a much lighter grey than the rest of its body. Three bluebottles were gorging on its blood and when we got closer one flew off as if it had had the fright of its life, but then immediately flew back to join the others. All three were jet black, with blue and red juices like the devil himself as Joe used to say, and they gorged on the dead animal like the devil himself, as Joe used to put it, even though he wore his bluebottle disguise. But their faces were black and Joe had said flames lit up the devil's face even though he wore a bluebottle's disguise. And his hands as well. So he was never mistaken for a real bluebottle. And when Anthony saw we found the rat so fascinating, he swooped on it and the trap, went into the street and threw the lot down the drain.

The kids were all over Anthony, after I'd been so afraid they'd hate the sight of him. Particularly my son; the girl was different, she was more reserved. But when Tony didn't have any schoolwork, he would always hover around Anthony and if Anthony told him to do something, he always did it very willingly. And if Anthony was reading the newspaper after dinner, my son would move closer and closer and would crawl all over him on the excuse that he also wanted to read the newspaper.

XLII

I lived shut up at home. The street frightened me. As soon as I poked my nose outside, the people, cars, buses and motorbikes terrified me … I turned tail. I was only happy at home. Although I found it an effort, I was making the house and its contents mine. And the shadow and the light. I knew where it was light during the day and where the patches of sun came through the bedroom and sitting-room balconies: when they were long and short. And the children celebrated their First Communion. We all wore new clothes. Mrs Enriqueta helped me dress my daughter. While I washed her all over in eau de cologne, I said look, how straight-backed she is … and Mrs Enriqueta said, if only we could rub her back with a drop of oil. We put on her dress and veil and Mrs Enriqueta, her mouth full of pins, pinned the veil and tiara to her hair. Once dressed, Rita looked like a doll. We had a party at home and after the party I went into her bedroom and helped her undress and, while she was folding her petticoat neatly on the bed, she said the father of a friend of hers at school who'd also taken her First

Communion that morning had fought in the war and he'd been posted dead but had come back two days ago, very sick, but alive, and they'd never found out because he'd been imprisoned a long way away and not been allowed to write letters ... And I turned slowly round and watched the way she looked at me and I realised how much she'd changed in all that time I'd been struggling to adapt to my new life. Rita was Joe. She had his monkey eyes and that something which you couldn't explain but looked as if it boded ill. And that's when my anxiety attacks started and I began sleeping badly, not sleeping, let alone living.

If Joe weren't dead, he'd be back. Who could actually tell us they'd seen him dead? No one. It was true enough that the watch they'd brought me was his, but it might have fallen into other hands and we'd believed he was dead because of a watch that was probably found on a wrist that wasn't Joe's. What if he was alive like the father of Rita's friend and came back sick and found I'd married the birdseed grocer? I couldn't think about anything else. When the kids weren't at home and Anthony was serving customers in the shop, I would pace up and down the passage as if it had been made especially for me before anyone knew I would need somewhere to pace up and down: from the sitting-room balcony to the Japanese woman in the dining-room, from the Japanese woman to the sitting-room balcony. Go into my son's bedroom? A wall. Go into the lavatory in the store? A wall. It was all walls, passages and bamboo Japanese woman curtain, wall after wall and passage after wall after passage and me pacing up and down thinking about things and every now and then entering one of the kids' rooms and hammering on the wall, and then into the other's and more hammering, and up and down again, and more walls. And opening and shutting drawers. When the cleaning lady finished washing the dishes and was going home, she'd say cloyingly, see you tomorrow, Madam Natalia, and I'd go into the kitchen. Another wall. And that tap. And water trickled from the tap and my finger sliced the trickle this way and that, like the wiper wiping a windscreen when it's raining, for half an hour, three quarters of an hour, an hour … without a clue as to what I was doing. Until my arm was aching and that took my mind off the sight of Joe coming back from travelling the world, perhaps just out of prison and straight back home and climbing the stairs. And he'd find other people in the flat and go down and ask the grocer what had happened, and the grocer downstairs would say I'd married the birdseed grocer because we thought he'd died in the war and Joe would turn up and set fire to everything. And the man who'd fought in the war would find he had no flat, no wife and no children. Just out of prison. He'd seem as ill as ever … Because I always believed him when he said he was ill. And if a slight draught rustled the bamboo curtain and the Japanese woman and I was standing with my back to her, I'd turn round, scared and tired, and I'd be thinking it must be him. And I might as well go after him and tell him, no worries, I'd only ever been married to him … after a couple of hidings I'd be lambasted for good. And this fear lasted two or three years. Perhaps a little longer or a little less, because things get hazy … and Mrs Enriqueta got into the bad habit of talking about Joe the minute we were by ourselves, do you remember when he used to go off with the boy on the motorbike? And what he said when the boy was born and what he said when Rita was born and what he said when he called you Pidgey? Do you remember that? Do you remember this?

I had to force myself to go out of the house because I wasn't eating or sleeping. I must go for walks. And think about other things. Everyone said I needed some fresh air. Because I lived as if I was shut up in prison ... The first day I went out with Rita after not going out for so long, the smell of the street made me feel dizzy. We went window-shopping down the High Street. We walked very slowly and when we got there Rita looked at me and said my eyes looked really scared. And I said I was seeing things. And we window-shopped and it made no difference ... And Rita wanted to cross over when we reached the bottom and walk back up the other side. And when I stepped on the edge of the kerb, the whole world seemed to cloud over and I saw blue lights, a good dozen at least, like a sea of blue blobs swirling in front of my eyes. And I fell down. And they had to carry me home. At night, when I was feeling better, while we were having dinner, Rita said I don't know what we're going to do because she faints when it's time to cross the street. And she said my eyes looked panic-stricken. And everybody said it was because I'd been shut up at home too long, and I'd have to force myself to go out a little at a time. And I did go out, but in other directions. And I began to walk in the parks, all alone.

XLIII

I watched lots of leaves fall and lots of buds open. One day, we're having lunch, Rita comes and says she wants to learn languages and only languages, so she can work for an aeroplane company. And be one of those girls who travel in planes and help passengers fasten their seatbelts so they don't shoot into the air, and bring them drinks and put pillows behind their heads. And Anthony, no sooner has Rita said all this, goes yes. That night I told Anthony that before saying yes he and I should discuss and decide whether it was a good idea for Rita to work aboard planes and he said perhaps it might have been a good idea for us to discuss it first, but if Rita was set on flying, we'd not budge her however much we warned her of the dangers. He said it's better to let young people be, because they are much more knowledgeable than us old 'uns, who walk backwards like crabs. And he said he'd been meaning to mention something to me for a long time, and if he hadn't, it was because I didn't seem to be one for talking a lot, but as we were chatting about Rita, he just felt he must tell me he'd never been so happy as when the three of us had come to live with him, and he wanted to thank me because with the happiness and luck I had brought him, things were going well even if they weren't as good as they used to be before. And he said all the money he had was for us. And fell asleep.

And I didn't know if I was asleep or awake, but I was seeing pigeons. I was seeing *them* as they used to be. Everything was exactly the same: the pigeon loft painted dark blue, the nesting boxes stuffed with esparto grass, the clothes lines on the terrace rusting because you couldn't hang anything out, the trapdoor, the pigeons parading from the back balcony to the one over the street after tripping through the whole flat ... It was all the same, but it was all lovely. These were pigeons that didn't make dirt, that didn't breed fleas, that only flew through the air above like God's angels. They raced in a flash of light and wing over the rooftops ... Their chicks were born covered in feathers, with no veins, with no tubes on their sad little necks, heads and beak in perfect proportion to their bodies. And their parents didn't stuff their food into them in a feverish rush and the chicks didn't cheep despairingly as they swallowed. And if an egg that was hatching fell on the floor it didn't stink. I looked after them and gave them fresh esparto. The water in their troughs didn't turn murky when it was hot ...

And the next morning, I described all that to a lady who sat down next to me on a bench in the park, in front of the rose garden. I told her I once owned forty pigeons ... forty pairs of pigeons: eighty ... Every sort. Silk-tie pigeons and pigeons with feathers turned upwards as if they'd been born in an upside-down world ... Croppers, fantails ... white, red, black and speckled ... with cowls, mantillas ... and ruffs of feathers from head to beak that covered their eyes ... and coffee-coloured spots ... They all lived in a tower that had been purpose built, climbed in via a spiralling ramp, and the sloping sides of the tower had long, narrow windows and inside under each small window was a nesting box with a broody pigeon. And the one waiting to take over perched on the window ledge, and if you looked at the tower from a good distance away, it looked like a high column covered in pigeons that seemed sculpted from stone but were for real. And they never flew off from the windows but always from the very top of the tower, and they took off like a streamer of feathers and beaks, but it was bombed in the war and that was the end of that.

That lady told another lady. And that lady, someone else. And they whispered in other ears and when they saw me coming, one always told the others, that is the pigeon lady. And now and then someone who'd yet to hear the whole story would ask, were they killed in the war? And another woman told the woman next to her on the park bench, now she says she can't think about anything else ... And another told the women who didn't know, her husband built her a tower so she could fill it with pigeons and it was like a cloud blessed with glory ... And when they talked about me, they said, she misses her pigeons, she misses her pigeons, the missus with the pigeons who lives longing for her pigeons and her tower with the little windows from top to bottom ...

And when I went to the parks I avoided the streets with too many cars because I got dizzy and sometimes I went round the houses, so I walked down quiet streets. And I had two or three routes so I didn't doze off always on the same roads. And I'd stop in front of houses I liked and look hard at them and, if I shut my eyes, I knew every detail by heart. And if I saw an open window with nobody inside, I'd look in. And as I walked along I'd think,

I wonder if the window with the black piano will be open, if the candlelit lobby will be open, or I'd wonder if the concierge in the white marble lobby had put his pots of greenery in the street to water, or wonder if the mansion with the front garden and blue-tiled fountain had switched the jet on ... But on days when it rained I stayed at home and I'd get into a state, so in the end I'd go out when it was raining and there'd be no ladies in the park and I'd take a newspaper and even if it was only a fine drizzle, I'd spread the paper on the bench and sit on it with my umbrella open and watch the rain streaming off the petals or the flowers opening and closing ... And I'd go home and sometimes get caught in a heavy downpour, but that was all right, I liked it, even. I was never in a hurry to get back and if I happened to walk by the marble entrance with the pots of greenery in the street so the rain watered them, I always stopped and stared for a while and I knew which leaves were in what pot and knew the ones they'd pruned when new leaves started to grow. And I'd walk along deserted streets and lived in easy-does-it fashion ... And I spent so long in one dreamy spell or another that I became a big softy and everything made me cry. And I always kept a little handkerchief tucked up my sleeve.

XLIV

One evening, when my son was heading off to his bedroom, Anthony asked him to stay with us for a while, he'd like to talk to him. I'd already cleared the table and put the tablecloth on with the vase in the middle with the circle of veiled ladies with long tresses, and the flowers I'd changed a long time ago for tulips and almond branches because the roses and daisies had faded and were covered in grime. Anthony said he'd like to know if the boy had thought about what he wanted to do when he grew up, and that perhaps, as he was a studious lad and doing well at school, he might like to go to university and start thinking about what profession he'd study for. He should take his time, no need to answer straight away, no point in rushing. The boy looked at the floor and listened and, when Anthony finished, he looked up, first at me and then at Anthony, and said there was nothing to think about because he'd made up his mind long ago. He said he didn't want to go to university, that he was studying to learn things that you need to know, because you do need to study and he was pleased to be doing so and to be getting that knowledge, but he was a practical sort and didn't want to leave home and all he asked was for Anthony to let him follow in his footsteps as a grocer, because, he went on, you're not getting any younger and you will need more and more help from me. Anthony had taken a lump of moss and was rolling it into a little ball. And he replied, I'd like to make one thing very clear: being a grocer is a job that ensures you don't go hungry, but it hardly gives you an opportunity to shine.

And he went on, still kneading that ball of moss between his fingers, perhaps the boy was just saying that to make him happy and he saw it as the beginning, not the end, of the conversation and he could take as long as he needed to think it over. Later on he didn't want him to regret pledging himself to the grocery store just to please him. And that he, Anthony-dad, had long realised my son had the brains to do whatever he wanted. Tony clenched his lips tight all the time he was listening, with two big creases between his eyebrows. He was so stubborn. And he said he knew only too well what he was saying and doing and why. And he repeated himself at least twice and in the end he blew up, and he was usually so placid and obedient. He blew up, and before he did that he also took a lump of moss, nervously, making all the flowers shake, and now they were both kneading little balls of moss. And he said that if he'd decided to be a grocer it was because he wanted to help Anthony-dad and carry on doing what he did and develop the shop further, because he really liked that shop. Abruptly he said good night and went into his bedroom. And when we were walking down the passage, on our way to bed, Anthony kept repeating himself as if he couldn't stop himself ... I don't deserve this ... I don't deserve this ... but he still said the boy was being silly and that he'd have been proud to see him a doctor or an architect and to think he'd helped him on his way.

We always undressed behind the screen so the bedroom chairs weren't piled high with clothes all night. There was a stool behind the screen for when we took our shoes off, and a hanger. Anthony would appear in his pyjamas and, before or afterwards, I'd also come out in my nightshirt, buttoning it to the neck and buttoning the sleeves. At the start, Anthony told me this habit of undressing behind the screen came from his mother. The material the screen was made of was crinkly from top to bottom and was held in place by small brass bars you removed when taking it out to wash. It was an expanse of sky blue with what looked like a scattering of white daisies.

At night I slept lightly, though I did sleep, and I'd be woken up by the first cart going to market and I'd get up for a glass of water and when I'd had a drink I'd listen out to make sure the kids were sound asleep, and as I didn't know what to do with myself, I'd walk through the Japanese woman and round the shop. I'd put my hand in the sacks of grain. In the sack of maize rather than the others because it was the one nearest the dining-room. I'd put my hand in and take out a handful of white-tipped yellow seeds and lift my hand up and open it and all the seeds fell like rain and I'd grab more and then sniff my hand and smell all kinds of smells. And in the brightness from the kitchen light I'd switched on, I could see the glass glinting on the fronts of the small drawers of pastas for soup, the tiny sort – little stars, letters of the alphabet – and millet and peppercorns. And the gleaming glass jars contained green olives and black olives that were all wrinkled as if they were a hundred years old. And I stirred them with the wooden spoon that was like an oar and made foam at the side of the jar. And the air reeked of olives. And, when I was concentrating like that, I sometimes thought that after all those years Joe must be dead, well and truly dead,

Joe who'd been as sharp as quicksilver, making designs for furniture in the strawberry lamplight in our dining-room ... and I thought how I didn't even know where he'd died or whether they'd buried him, far, far away ... or whether he was still above ground, the wind blowing over his bones in the parched grass of the Aragonese desert, or whether the wind was burying them in dust, except for the ribs that were hollowed out like an empty cage where once it was full of pink lung perforated with holes that kept growing and nasty bugs. And the ribs were all there except for one that was me, and when I broke from the rib cage, I immediately picked a small blue flower and plucked its petals off and the petals swirled through the air like maize seed. And all the flowers were blue, the colour of sea, river or spring water, and all the leaves were green like the snake hiding there with an apple in its big mouth. And when I picked the flower and plucked its petals off, Adam slapped me on the hand, don't spoil things! And the snake couldn't laugh because it had to hold the apple and follow me on the sly ... And I was falling asleep again and I switched off the kitchen light and the cart had gone by some time ago and more carts and lorries kept coming, all going down, down, down ... and sometimes so many wheels turning distracted me and I'd fall asleep again ...

XLV

'There's a young man here wanting to talk to you,' said
Anthony, from just outside the sitting room. Rosa was ironing
and I was sitting on the settee with the overlay. He added that
the young man had come to inform him of something but he'd
told him to wait a moment because I was the person he really
needed to speak to. I thought it was a bit odd. I told Rosa I'd
be back straight away. Don't worry, Madam Natalia. I was very
curious and went to the dining-room and in the passage
Anthony told me the young man who wanted to see me must
be the best-looking in the whole district. I was almost in a faint
when I reached the dining-room where I found the owner of
the bar on the corner. He was quite a newcomer because he
only bought the bar two years ago. Anthony was right, the bar-
owner was very good-looking: well built, with hair as black
as a blackbird's wing. And very nice. As soon as he saw me
he said he was the old-fashioned sort. I told him to sit down
and we sat down. Anthony left and the lad started talking. He
said he had one vice, work. I'm very hardworking. He said the

bar-cum-restaurant gave him enough to live on and save, even though times were hard, and next year he was going to buy the soap-maker's shop next door which he'd been negotiating for some time, and would extend the bar and the function room. And in three or four years this extension would earn him enough to buy a little house in Cadaqués, next to where his parents lived, because when he was married he wanted his wife to enjoy good summer holidays by the seaside and he thought the sea was one of the loveliest things in the whole world.

'I have very loving parents and was always happy and well looked after at home. If I marry, I want my wife to be able to say what my father says about my mother, and I've only ever heard him say one thing: "It was my lucky day when I met you!"'

I listened, not saying anything, because the lad was like a millstream in full flood, and who knew where this was leading. And when he shut up, he shut up. And I waited and waited and finally got a word out after a very long silence, 'You mean . . .'

And that was it. Rita.

'Whenever I see her walk by, it's like looking at a flower. And I've come to ask for her hand.'

I got up, put my head through the bamboo curtain and called to Anthony and he came and I was going to fill him in and he said no need and he sat down as well. I said Rita hadn't said a word to me and we'd have to wait for her to decide. And he said, call me Vincent. And he added that Rita knew nothing. I told him the first thing I should do was talk to Rita, but *he* should realise she was very young. He said he wasn't worried about her being very young, he'd wait if she wanted to wait, though he was ready to marry her tomorrow morning, and didn't even need to talk to her, he was an old-fashioned sort and wouldn't dare, and we ought to talk to her and see what she said. Ask around about me, if you want. I said I'd talk to Rita, but my daughter could be very bad-tempered and perhaps we'd get nowhere doing it that way. No sooner said than done. When Rita came home, I told her the lad from the bar had come to ask for her hand in marriage. She looked at me and, instead of responding, she took her books into her bedroom, went into the kitchen to wash her hands and then came back and said, do you think I feel like getting married and being buried alive here as the wife of the man who owns the bar on the corner?

She sat down in the dining-room and twice swept her hair back and she looked at me and her eyes twinkled and all of a sudden she burst out laughing, could hardly get a word out, and now and again, when she could, she said, don't keep looking at me like that . . .

And her laughter was infectious and I burst out laughing as well, heaven knows why, and we both laughed loudly and Anthony came, separated out the bamboo and stuck his head inside without actually coming into the room and asked, what are you two laughing about? And when we saw him there we still couldn't stop laughing and finally Rita said, it was the big joke about the wedding, and she said she didn't want to get married, she wanted to see the world, and didn't want to get married, didn't want to get married and we could tell the bar-owner as much, no way and he was wasting his time and she had other things on her mind. And she asked, did he come to ask for my hand? And Anthony said he did and Rita burst out laughing again, ha, ha, ha, ha, and finally I said that was enough, it was hardly a laughing matter if a handsome lad wanted to make her his wife.

XLVI

Vincent came back, at Anthony's request, and I told him, sorry, Rita's obstinate and goes her own way. And he said, would you like me? We said we would, to which he replied, very politely, then Rita is going to be mine.

Flowers rained down and an invitation to dinner at his bar. Tony sided with Rita and said he didn't like Vincent one bit, that Rita was right, why should she get involved with the boy from the local bar if what she wanted was to see the world, and if the boy from the bar wanted to marry, the place was full of girls who'd fall over themselves to get him.

One morning Rita was in the entrance to the veranda and I'm not sure what I was doing in the sitting room but I was by the window looking out at her. She was facing the yard and had her back to me, and the sun was projecting her shadow over the ground, and her hair glinted and blew in the sunlight and she looked so lovely with her slim body and long, firm legs! She kept dragging the toe of her shoe across the ground, drawing a line in the dust.

Her foot shifted to and fro as she drew the line and all of a sudden I noticed I was standing on the shadow from Rita's head, or rather, the shadow from her head kept climbing up my feet, but even so, I kept thinking that Rita's shadow on the ground was like a lever and I might shoot into the air at any moment because the sun and Rita outside weighed much more than the shadow and myself inside. And I felt very keenly the time passing. Not the time of the clouds, sun and rain or the movement of the stars twinkling at night, not spring in springtime and autumn in autumn time, or what brings the leaves to branches or strips them off, or what opens and closes flowers, but the time within myself, the time we don't see, that shapes us. What goes round and round our heart and makes it beat, changing us inside and out, patiently preparing us for what we'll be like on the day we die. And while Rita was drawing that line in the dust with her toe, I could see her running around the dining-room chasing Tony and tottering in a flurry of pigeons ... And Rita turned and was surprised to see me standing there in the entrance to the sitting room, and she said she'd be back in a moment and left through the garden door. She came back a good half-hour later, cheeks flushed, and said she'd just seen Vincent and they'd quarrelled, because she'd told him the first thing a boy must do if he wants to marry a girl is to win her over and not go behind her back to her parents, and she also told him you don't send flowers to a girl without finding out, in advance, whether she'll be pleased to receive them. And I asked her what Vincent had said and he'd said he was really in love and if she didn't want him he'd shut his bar down and become a monk.

And we had dinner in Vincent's bar. Rita wore a sky-blue dress embroidered with white lozenges, spent the whole time sulking and didn't try a single thing. She said she wasn't hungry.

And finally, when it was time for desserts, when the waiter had finished flitting around us bringing the various courses, Vincent said, as if he was talking to himself, some lads have a way of winning girls over but I'm not one of them.

But he did just that with those words. And they started courting. A courtship that was like open battle. All of a sudden Rita would say the engagement was over and she didn't want to marry Vincent or anyone else. She'd shut herself up in her bedroom. She'd leave to go to her classes and the second she'd caught the bus, at the stop practically in front of Vincent's bar, he'd pay us a visit.

'I sometimes think she loves me and two days later I think she doesn't. I give her a flower and she's happy and two days after I give her another flower and she refuses to take it.'

Anthony came into the dining-room, sat down and picked up a bit of moss. I soothed Vincent, saying that Rita was very young, a kitten, and Vincent said he realised that and that was why he was being so patient but he was pining because he never knew where he stood with her. When it was almost time for Rita to come back, Vincent beat a swift retreat. Tony sometimes joined in the banter, and when he saw Vincent really was suffering, he was sad too. He gradually came round to Vincent and started arguing with Rita and defending him. What will you do after you've been round the world? he asked her.

When Anthony and our son talked about the shop and what they should buy and how they should organise their business, I'd sometimes leave them to it or I'd go in and out of the dining-room, tidying up, not listening. But one night I heard the word 'soldier' and that brought me to a standstill by the kitchen door as if I'd been nailed to the spot. And his father was saying he'd certainly be able to do his military service in Barcelona, and something or other about that meaning an extra year and Tony said he'd rather do an extra year and stay in Barcelona than do a year in some godforsaken spot. And he told his father he shouldn't find that odd, because, when he was a child, during the war, he'd had to spend time away from home because there was nothing to eat, and that had made him crazy to be home, always to be home, like a worm in the beam, and he'd always be obsessed that way and he'd never get over it. And his father said, I see what you mean. And I went into the dining-room, and the moment he saw me, Anthony said we'd soon be seeing our son in uniform.

XLVII

Rita fixed the wedding day when we were all there and said she was agreeing so as not to see Vincent so miserable and going round the neighbourhood acting the poor victim and looking for sympathy. And the mere expression on his face was enough to suggest to everyone that she was a nasty piece of work. And with the reputation he was giving her, if she didn't marry him, she'd be only good for the shelf, and it wasn't that she didn't like him, and, seeing as she couldn't do what she wanted and work on an aeroplane, she fancied the idea of dressing smartly and going to the cinema or theatre on the arm of a really handsome young man and she had to admit that Vincent was very good-looking. The only thing that bothered her, and it bothered her more than anything, was the fact that he was so local and his place was so close to home. We asked her why and she said it was hard to put into words, but she felt a bit downcast because marrying someone so close to home was like marrying a member of your family and hardly what she'd dreamed of. And the period for courting, for getting used to one another, seemed endless and spilled over into the wedding preparations. We got a dressmaker to come twice a week and turned the sitting room into a workroom. Vincent would pay us a visit while Rita and she were sewing. As soon as she saw him she got very up in arms and said if he didn't live round the corner he wouldn't be able to come and snoop like that. He'd find out what's what before he should ... Vincent knew what Rita was getting at but he couldn't stop himself and he'd come into the sitting room as if he were committing a sin and stand there for a while and, when he saw we were all hard at work, he'd turn tail, and finally I did too and let Rita and the dressmaker get on with the wedding dress because Rita didn't think much of my sewing. And I went off to the park, which I'd grown tired of, tired of those ladies I knew would be waiting for me with pitying expressions because I'd once owned pigeons. And the misery I felt before when I used to talk about the pigeons and their tower had faded over time.

If I felt like thinking about the pigeons, I preferred to do so by myself. And to think about them as I wanted. Sometimes it made me sad and sometimes it didn't. And depending on the day, sitting under those leafy branches, I'd feel like a good giggle because I could see myself killing the chicks in their eggs. And if I left home with an umbrella because it was cloudy and spotted a bird feather in the park I'd spear it with the tip of my umbrella and bury it deep in the ground. And if I bumped into one of those ladies who knew me and she said, why don't you sit down next to me? I'd say I don't know what's wrong but if I sit down I feel sick. And if the weather turned cool I'd say, if I sit down, all the damp from the leaves goes into my back and I start coughing at night ... And I'd stand there like that and have fun looking at the trees that lived with their legs up in the air, with all those leaves they had for feet. Trees living with their heads under the ground eating earth with mouths and teeth that were their roots. And their blood ran differently from people's blood: from the head to the feet along the top of the trunk. And the wind and rain and birds tickled the feet of the trees that were so green when they were born. So yellow when dying.

And I'd come home feeling a bit queasy as usual because I didn't know why but the fresh air affected me badly and as soon as I walked into the living room I'd find the lights all on, Rita grumbling and the dressmaker looking upset and Vincent standing or sitting, or not there at all. And Anthony always asked me if I had had a good walk. And sometimes Tony was there watching Rita and the dressmaker sewing or else he was shouting at Rita because he was starving after doing a stint as a soldier and Rita didn't want to get him a bite to eat because she said if she wasted time her clothes would never be ready for the wedding and she wanted it all over and done with and didn't want to sew ever again and the second she was married she only wanted to live her life and enjoy herself. Sometimes I'd find them all eating an afternoon snack and arguing about this, that or the other. And when I got there, I'd change my shoes immediately and sit on the settee and while they were talking I'd still be seeing leaves, dead or alive, ones that grew and rustled on branches and those that curled silently through the air like the lightest pigeon feather.

XLVIII

And the wedding day came. It had rained all night and was still pouring when it was time to go to church. Rita wore a bridal gown because I wanted her to, because a good wedding is a wedding where the bride dresses as a bride. And we held the wedding to coincide with the anniversary of my marriage to Anthony. Mrs Enriqueta, who was ageing fast, made Rita a wedding present of the locust picture, because you were always looking at it when you were little ... Anthony handed over a lot of cash so she wasn't a girl without a dowry. Vincent said he wasn't expecting that, although he was grateful, but he would marry Rita with or without a dowry, and Rita said the dowry would come in useful when she separated from Vincent. When Rita married, she had everything. We organised lunch in Vincent's bar, in the function room, which he'd extended when he'd bought the soap-maker's some time ago and changed it lock, stock and barrel, and there were garlands of asparagus fern on the walls with white paper roses, because real ones were over by now. And they had hung paper roses from the lights on long ribbons and then there were the small red lamps they'd switched on, though it was daytime. The waiters could hardly move their shirts were so stiff with starch. Vincent's parents came from Cadaqués, dressed in black with beautifully polished shoes, and my children and Vincent and Anthony insisted I wore a champagne-coloured silk dress. And I wore a long necklace of cultured pearls. Vincent's face was pallid and drained because he'd finally made it after saying for so long that he never would, and it was as if he'd been murdered and then forced to rise from the dead. Rita was in a temper because her train and veil got wet when she came out of church. Tony couldn't come to the ceremony but did come to the lunch and dance in his military uniform. And when we had to switch on the fans, the draught made the paper roses flutter. And Rita danced with Anthony and Anthony was as soft and soggy as a rotten peach. And Vincent's parents, who'd never met me, said they were extremely happy to make my acquaintance and I said I too was extremely happy to make theirs and they said Vincent was always mentioning Rita and Madam Natalia in his letters. After three dances Rita took off her veil which she said was a nuisance when you were dancing and danced with everybody and laughed when she danced and threw her head back and held her dress up and her eyes sparkled and small pearls of sweat glistened between her nose and top lip. And when Rita danced with Anthony, Mrs Enriqueta, who was wearing earrings with lilac-coloured gems, came over and said, if only Joe could see her now ... And people came and said hello to me and I hardly recognised them and they said, how are you, Madam Natalia ... ? And when I danced with my son the soldier, the palm of my hand and the skin that spreads from my wrist to my fingers pressed against the palm of my son's hand, and I felt as if the column on the bed made from the small balls one on top of the other was breaking, and my hand dropped from his and I put it on his neck and squeezed and he said, what are you doing? and I said, I'm strangling you. And when I finished that dance with my son, the pearl necklace caught on a button on his soldier's jacket and the pearls scattered and everybody started picking them up and handing them to me, saying, here you are, here you are, here you are, Madam Natalia, and I put them in my handbag, here you are, here you are ... I waltzed with Anthony and everyone formed a circle to watch us because, before we started whirling round, Anthony had announced that we were celebrating our wedding anniversary. And Rita came over and kissed me. And she whispered to me, while Vincent was announcing the waltz, that she'd fallen madly in love with Vincent from that first day, but she'd not wanted to show it and Vincent would never know how much she was in love with him. And as she said that, her lips brushed against me and I felt her hot breath on my cheeks. The party was winding down and it would soon be time to call it a day. Tony went off, the newlyweds left, and before they did so Rita gave flowers to some people. It was so hot inside but outside it was a cool, pink evening that felt like the end of summer. The rain was only spotting but the whole street smelled of rain. Anthony and I went home, and in through the door to the yard. I undressed behind the screen and Anthony said I should rethread my necklace with a thread that didn't break so easily and he also changed his clothes and went into the shop to tidy up. I sat on the settee opposite the console. I could see the top of my head in the console mirror, and a bit of hair, and those flowers from heaven knows how many years ago were still slumbering in the bell jars, on both sides. The conch-shell was in the middle of the console, and I felt I could hear the sea roaring inside ... boom ... boom ... and I thought that perhaps when nobody was listening, there was no sound inside, and that it was something you could never know, whether waves crashed in the conch-shell when no ear was there to listen. I took the pearls out of my handbag and put them in a box and kept one back which I threw inside the conch-shell to keep the sea company. I went to ask Anthony if he wanted any dinner and he said, a cup of white coffee will do, thank you very much. And as I'd asked him from out in the passage, he'd come into the dining-room to tell me and when he'd told me he went back to the shop through the bamboo curtain and I went back to the settee until it got dark and I was in the dark, until they switched on the street lights and a dim glow came in from the street and gave the red tiles a ghostly white hue. I took the conch-shell and very slowly shook it this way and that, so I could hear the pearl inside. It was pink, with patches of white, little spikes and a blunt spike at the end and mother-of-pearl inside. I put it back where it had always been kept and thought how the conch-shell was a church and the pearl was Father John and boom ... boom ... a song sung by angels who only knew how to sing that one song. And I sat back on the settee where I stayed until Anthony came and asked what I was doing sitting there in the dark and I said I wasn't doing anything in particular. And he asked me if I was thinking about Rita and I said I was, though I wasn't. And he sat down next to me and said why don't we go to bed early because his whole body was aching because he wasn't used to wearing a waistcoat and I said I was tired too and we got up and I went to make his cup of white coffee and he said, half a cup will do ...

XLIX

Tony woke me up when he came home, even though he always tiptoed across the yard when it was late at night. I started to run a finger across one of the crocheted flowers and a petal stretched. A piece of furniture creaked, perhaps it was the console, or the settee, or the chest of drawers ... and in the dark I saw the bottom of Rita's white dress swirling over her satin shoes and diamond-studded buckles. And night-time went on and on. There was a heart at the centre of each of the roses on the counterpane and, once, one of the hearts got frayed and a tiny button jumped out ... Madam Natalia. I got up. Tony had left the balcony on the latch so as not to wake us up ... I went to shut the balcony. And when I was almost there I went back to our bedroom and groped my way to behind the screen and dressed in the pitch black. And it was still the early hours. I crept to the kitchen, as usual, barefoot and keeping close to the walls. I stopped by the door to my son's bedroom and listened to him breathing hard and peacefully. And, out of sheer habit, went into the kitchen to drink a glass of water. I opened the drawer of the white table with the small-check oilskin tablecloth and took out the potato-peeling knife which had a very sharp point. The blade was serrated like a saw ... Madam Natalia. Whoever had invented that knife had made a very good job of it. He must have been racking his brains for a long time somewhere after dinner under a light over a table because knives used to be different and needed a knife-grinder and perhaps the man who'd burnt the midnight oil inventing that serrated edge was to blame for forcing knife-grinders to find another trade. Perhaps the wretched grinders did something else now, made more money in another trade and streaked their motorbikes up and down the road like lightning frightening their wives. Up and down the road. Because it was all the same: roads, streets, passages and houses where you lived like a worm in a lump of wood. Walls and yet more walls. Once Joe happened to say woodworms were really bad luck and I replied I couldn't understand how they breathed, boring one hole after another like that, and the more they bored the less they breathed and he said they were made that way, with their noses toiling away in the wood, good workers that they were. And I thought how perhaps knife-grinders could still make a living from their trade because not all knives were kitchen knives or knives for hospices and children's camps, where those in charge only thought about scrimping, and people still owned knives with blades that needed a grindstone from time to time. And while I was thinking those thoughts, the smell and the stench began. Every kind. Chasing each other, finding a space, disappearing, then coming back: the smell of our terrace with and without pigeons and the stench of bleach, a stench I really discovered when I got married. And the smell of blood heralding the smell of death. And the smell of sulphur from the rockets and bangers that time in Diamond Square and the paper smell of paper roses and the dry smell of the asparagus fern which was crumbling on to the ground and making a mess with the tiny, tiny green bits that fell off its branches. And the smell of the sea that was so strong. And I wiped my hand over my eyes. And I wondered why smells were called smells and stench stench and why couldn't smells be stench and stench be smells and then I got a whiff of Anthony's smell when he was awake and when he was asleep. And I told Joe that rather than working from the outside in perhaps the worms went from the inside out and stuck their heads out of the little holes they made and thought about the damage they were doing. And the smell of small kids, of milk and dribble, of milk that was fresh and milk that had gone sour. And Mrs Enriqueta once told me we live many lives and they all get entangled, and a death or a wedding couldn't always untangle them, and that real life, free from the threads of petty lives that had twisted round it, could be lived as it should be lived providing petty and ne'er-do-well lives left it alone. And she went on, these entangled lives quarrel and torment us and we don't know it's happening, just as we don't know how our heart works or how our intestines cope ... And the smell of sheets full of my body and Anthony's, that smell of old sheets that suck in someone's smell, the smell of hair on the pillow, the smell from all the little bits feet leave at the end of the bed, the smell from yesterday's clothes hanging on the back of a chair overnight ... And the smell of grain and potatoes and from the cylinder of spirit of salts ... The knife's wooden handle was held in place by three small nails, the heads of which had been hammered flat, so it could never be detached from the blade. I was carrying my shoes and when I went into the yard I left the veranda door ajar as if driven by a force that didn't come from inside or out, and I leaned on a pillar so as not to fall down when I put my shoes on ... I thought I heard the first cart of the morning away in the distance, still half lost somewhere in the night that was drawing to a close ... Shining in the light from the street lamp large numbers of leaves rustled on the peach tree and birds flew out. A branch shook. The sky was a dark blue and on the other side of the street the roofs of the two blocks with facing balconies were silhouetted against the dark blue that was so high up in the sky. I was thinking how I had done everything I had ever done not knowing where I was or when, as if it were all planted and rooted in a time that had no memory ... And I touched my face and it *was* my face, my skin and my nose and the curve of my cheek and although it was me I saw these things in a haze, though they weren't dead, as if they'd been hidden under cloud after cloud of dust ... I swung left, towards the High Street, before the market and further down than the emporium with the dolls. And when I was in the High Street I walked along the pavement, racing from one flagstone to the next, until I reached the long kerbstone where I stood as stiff as a board on the outside, but with a stack of things rushing from my heart to my head. A tram clattered by, it must have been the first out of the garage, a run-of-the-mill tram, like them all, battered and old; perhaps that tram had watched me running with Joe in hot pursuit, when we scampered like mad mice from Diamond Square. And I felt something irritating my neck like a pea rattling in my eardrum. I felt queasy and closed my eyes and the draught from the tram helped move me on as if my life depended on it. And with my first step I could still see the tram which was leaving a trail of red and blue sparks between its wheels and the rails. It was as if I was blindly walking above the abyss, thinking every second that I was about to fall, and I crossed to the other side gripping the knife tight and not seeing any blue lights ...

And once I was over I turned round and looked with my eyes and all my heart and thought it couldn't possibly be true. I had made it to the other side. And I started walking through my old life until I was opposite our old house, under the bay window ... The front door was shut. I looked up and saw Joe in the middle of a field near the sea, when I was pregnant with Anthony, and he was offering me a little blue flower and laughing at me. I wanted to go upstairs, back to my flat, to my terrace, to the scales and run my hand over them as I passed. I'd gone in through that door for years and years as Joe's wife and had left through it to marry Anthony trailing my kids behind me. The street was ugly, the building was ugly, and the paving was paving fit only for carts and horses. The street lamp was a long way away and the entrance was dingy. I looked for the hole Joe had made in the door, above the keyhole, and found it straight away: packed with cork right above the keyhole. I started scraping out bits of cork with the point of my knife. And the cork crumbled and fell out. And I removed it all and then I realised I couldn't go in. My fingers couldn't reach the string, in order to pull it and yank the door open. I should have brought a piece of wire to hook on to the string. And I was about to knock on the door but thought it would make too much noise and hit the wall instead and hurt myself badly. And I turned round and rested and felt it was very early in the morning. And I looked at the door and with the point of the knife carved out PIDGEY in deep grooves, and, not thinking, I started walking and followed the walls rather than my footsteps, and came to Diamond Square: a box of old houses with the sky for a lid. And I saw small shadows flying at the centre of the lid and the houses started rocking to and fro as if they'd been plunged into water and somebody was slowly stirring the water and the house walls began to stretch up and lean into each other and the lid space kept narrowing into a funnel. And I felt a hand in mine and it was Matthew's and a satin-tie pigeon settled on his shoulder, the like of which I'd never seen before, a rainbow sheen on its feathers, and I heard a stormy wind gusting around the funnel that was almost closed by now and I put my arms over my face to save me from whatever was about to happen and let out a scream from hell. A scream I must have been carrying deep inside me for years and a little something else ran from my mouth alongside that scream that was so vast it was hard to get out of my throat, like a cockroach made from saliva, and that little something else that had been shut up inside me for so long was my youth that now rushed out screaming something or other ... that I'd been forsaken? Someone touched my arm and I turned round, and wasn't scared one bit, and an old man asked me if I was ill and I heard a balcony open, aren't you feeling well? And an old woman came over and the old couple stood in front of me and I could see a white shadow on the balcony. I'm all right now, I replied. And more people came, slowly, like the light of day, and I said that was that, it was all over, it was nerves, nothing to worry about ... And I started walking again, back the same way. I turned round to look at the old couple, who still stood rooted to the spot, staring after me, and in the dim light of early dawn they seemed unreal ... Thank you. Thank you. Thank you. Anthony had spent years saying thank you and I'd never thanked him for anything. Thank you ... I stood on the kerbstone, looked up and down the High Street to make sure no trams were coming and ran across the street and when I was on the other side I turned round again to see if that little something else that had driven me crazy was still chasing me. And I was alone. Colour had been restored to houses and objects. Carts and lorries were going up and down the streets to the market and the men from the slaughterhouse were walking into the market, in bloodstained aprons, calves split down the middle slung over their shoulders. Flower-sellers were putting bunches in metal containers full of water, bunches of flowers that would be made into bouquets. The chrysanthemums gave off a bitter smell. The wasps' nest was coming back to life. And I went up my street, the one where the early morning cart always rolled by. And as I walked I peered into the big entrance where, years ago, a man sold peaches and pears and shit-shifting prunes, with old scales and brass and iron weights. He held the scales up in the air, the hook hanging from a finger. And the ground was strewn with straw, small piles of wood shavings and sheets of dirty, crumpled paper. No, thank you very much. And the last birds squawking high in the sky, before they made their escape, trembling in the tremulous blue. I stopped by the barred gate. The balconies rose up, one above another, like niches in a strange cemetery, with green blinds pulled up or down. Clothes on clothes lines and now and then a splash of colour that was a potted geranium. I entered the yard when a miserable sliver of sunbeam was speckling the leaves of the peach tree and Anthony was there waiting for me, nose pressed against the windowpane. And I deliberately walked very slowly, dragging my feet, and slowly ... my feet were guiding me and were feet that had covered a lot of ground and when I died perhaps Rita would hold them together with a safety pin. And Anthony opened the balcony and his voice shook as he asked me, what's wrong? and he said he'd been worrying a long time because he'd suddenly woken up as if he'd been made aware of some impending disaster and he'd not found me by his side or anywhere else. And I said, your feet will freeze ... and I'd woken up when it was still dark and hadn't been able to get back to sleep and had needed a breath of fresh air because there was something that was choking me ... He said nothing and went back to bed. There's still time to get some sleep, I said, and I watched him from the back, the hairs on the back of his neck grown too long, his ears white and forlorn that were always white when it was cold ... I put the knife on top of the console and started to undress. First I shut the shutters and the sun shone through a small chink and I went over to our bed, sat down, and took my shoes off. The mattress squeaked, because it was old and we should have changed two springs a long time ago. I pulled my stockings off as if I were pulling off a long piece of skin, put on some bedsocks, and then I realised how frozen I was. I put on a nightshirt that had faded from being washed so much. I buttoned it to the neck, straightened it and did the sleeve buttons up. I shook the shirt down to my feet, got into bed and tucked myself in. And said, it's a lovely day. The bed was as warm as a canary's belly, but Anthony was shivering. I heard his teeth chattering, top against bottom and vice versa. He had his back to me and I put my arm under his and hugged his chest. I was still cold. I wrapped my legs around his, and my feet around his, and put my hand down inside and undid his belt so he could breathe more easily. I pressed my cheek against his back, against his knobbly bones, and it was as if I could hear everything alive inside, that was also him: his heart, his lungs and his liver, all swimming in juices and blood. And I began to move my hand gingerly over his belly because he was my cripple and pressing my head against his back I thought how I didn't want him to die on me and I wanted to tell him everything I was thinking, that I thought more than I said, and thoughts you can't say, and said nothing and my feet were warming up and we went to sleep like that and before I fell asleep, when I was moving my hand over his belly, I touched his belly button and put my finger in and over it so he didn't empty out through there ... when we are born, we are all like pears ... so he wouldn't slide off like a stocking. So no witch could suck him dry through his belly button and take my Anthony away from me ... And we went to sleep like that, slowly, like two of God's angels, him until eight and me until well after twelve ... And when I woke up from that deep sleep, my mouth was parched and bitter-tasting, waking up after that night of nights on that morning that was midday and I got up and started to get dressed as usual, almost without thinking, as my spirit was still in sleep's cocoon. And when I was up on my feet, I held my hands to my temples and I knew I'd done something different but I found it hard to think what I'd done and whether I'd done whatever I'd done half awake or fast asleep, until I washed my face and the water woke me up ... and put colour in my cheeks and a sparkle in my eyes ... No point having breakfast because it was too late. Just drank a gulp of water to douse the fire in my mouth ... The water was cold and I remembered how the day before, on the morning of the wedding, it had poured down and I thought how that afternoon, when I went to the park as usual, I might still find puddles on the side paths ... and inside each puddle, however small, there would be a sky ... the sky a bird sometimes disturbed ... a thirsty bird disturbing the sky unawares with water from its beak ... or shrieking out of the foliage like flashes of lightning, several birds would swoop down for a quick bath in the puddle, ruffling their feathers and then wiping the mud, their beaks and their wings all over the sky. Happy ...

Geneva, February–September 1960

VIRAGO MODERN CLASSICS

The first Virago Modern Classic, *Frost in May* by Antonia White, was published in 1978. It launched a list dedicated to the celebration of women writers and to the rediscovery and reprinting of their works. Its aim was, and is, to demonstrate the existence of a female tradition in literature, and to broaden the sometimes narrow definition of a 'classic' which has often led to the neglect of interesting books. Published with new introductions by some of today's best writers, the books are chosen for many reasons: they may be great works of literature; they may be wonderful period pieces; they may reveal particular aspects of women's lives; they may be classics of comedy, storytelling, letter-writing or autobiography.

'The Virago Modern Classics list is wonderful. It's quite simply one of the best and most essential things that has happened in publishing in our time. I hate to think where we'd be without it'
Ali Smith

'A continuingly magnificent imprint'
Joanna Trollope

'The Virago Modern Classics have reshaped literary history and enriched the reading of us all. No library is complete without them'
Margaret Drabble

'The writers are formidable, the production handsome. The whole enterprise is thoroughly grand'
Louise Erdrich

'The Virago Modern Classics are one of the best things in Britain today'
Alison Lurie

Good news for everyone writing and reading today'
Hilary Mantel

'Masterful works'
Vogue

MARY LAVELLE

Kate O'Brien

Introduced by Michèle Roberts

Mary Lavelle, a beautiful young Irish woman, travels to
Spain to see some of the world before marrying her steadfast
fiancé John. But despite the enchanting surroundings and
her three charming charges, life as governess to the wealthy
Areavaga family is lonely and she is homesick. Then comes
the arrival of the family's handsome, passionate – and
married – son Juanito, and Mary's loyalties and beliefs are
challenged. Falling in love with Juanito and with Spain, Mary
finds herself at the heart of a family and a nation divided.

'She writes with almost poetic intensity of
the ecstacy and anguish of love'
Val Hennessy

'A superior type of romantic novel ...
colourful and unorthodox'
Times Literary Supplement

virago

To buy any of our books and to find out more
about Virago Press and Virago Modern Classics,
our authors and titles, as well as events and
book club forum, visit our websites

www.virago.co.uk
www.littlebrown.co.uk

and follow us on Twitter

@ViragoBooks

To order any Virago titles p & p free in the UK,
please contact our mail order supplier on:

+ 44 (0)1832 737525

Customers not based in the UK should contact
the same number for appropriate postage
and packing costs.